BYRON'S DIARY

BYRON'S DIARY

A Novella

Julian Fane

The Book Guild Ltd
Sussex, England

First published in Great Britain in 2003 by
The Book Guild Ltd
25 High Street
Lewes, East Sussex
BN7 2LU

Typesetting in Garamond by
Keyboard Services, Luton, Bedfordshire

Printed in Great Britain by
Antony Rowe Ltd, Chippenham, Wiltshire

A catalogue record for this book is available from
The British Library

ISBN 1 85776 715 2

To
All the Fanes, dead and alive

CONTENTS

EXPLANATION

The story begins in the 1950s, roughly fifty years ago. I was then in my twenties and writing my first essay in prose, its working title *Scenes from Childhood*. Somebody suggested that I should send a chapter to the old-established publishing house John Murray in hopes of getting it into Murray's quarterly magazine, *The Cornhill*. I did so and it was rejected; but not rejected in the modern manner, with a chilly printed slip that often adds insult to injury by wishing aged scribblers good luck with their writing, and not even after several months delay, but promptly, in a gracious letter signed by John Grey Murray in person, who invited me to be sure to let him see the completed work.

I had been writing plays full-time for five or six years before turning towards a book; rejection was therefore no stranger to me, but the politeness of the Murray sort, an exception to the general rule even in those less thuggish days, bowled me over. Far from being cast down, I was buoyed up by the encouragement and impatient to accept the invitation. My book was finished as books are, that is eventually, and, in short, I became a Murray author.

John Grey Murray, Jock to me after we met and became business partners, continued to be unfailingly polite, but did advance a couple of ideas that shocked me. He was a nice-looking slim forty-year-old in a bow-tie at that time, and was unusual again in asking me what I thought of his ideas instead of thrusting them down my throat in the pill-like form of 'improvements'. He wondered if I would like to add another chapter or chapters to my book to show the reader what happened to my characters – my answer no doubt betrayed my horror before such a prospect. His next question was worse from my point of view: should my book, now retitled *Morning*, be issued as fiction or autobiography?

For two reasons, or two and a half, Jock had touched a sensitive spot. I had found out in my school days that I was a dreamer, a rearranger of reality, a would-be story-teller; and had thought and hoped that readers of *Morning* would see the point that the text was as true as possible in an emotional sense, but not photographic, nor exactly about myself. Jock's uncertainty was dis-illusioning, to say the least. My second reason for wincing was sociological and calls for another paragraph.

Inverted snobbery was getting a grip on our country. Communism had instigated class war, and World War II fanned the flames of egali-tarianism. The spirit of the age in England did not tempt the new establishment to chop off a second royal head or to behave so cruelly as the French and the Russians had done. Instead, it discriminated increasingly against 'toffs'. Unless you were a commoner, unless you were common for that matter, you got nowhere. An Oxford accent was an unloved thing. Public school products were low on the lists of possible employees. Better-off people were only forgiven if they were entertainers. Gentlemen were frowned on and peers of the realm were fit for nothing but the scrap heap. And literature was being downgraded as elitist, and the heroes of the critical fraternity were the Angry Young Men, whose nihilism made some of them rich and famous.

The consequent problem for me as I responded to my vocation was that I happened to be a minor sprig of the aristocracy: how was I to present myself to the prejudiced levellers who might read me, and what was I to write about if not the world I had been born into?

To be more precise, I was the second son of the 14th Earl of Westmorland. The meaning of my birth in down-to-earth terms was that after my elder brother had sired heirs to the title I was a nobody, and, since my forebears had managed to lose nearly all they once possessed, cash was in short supply until Dame Fortune smiled on me in late middle age. But, thanks to my service as a private soldier in the army, I was aware that my countrymen in general were against their officers, against anyone tainted by any sort of superiority, although they were ignorant of, and had not the slightest interest in, how our social system worked and why it had done so for hundreds of years. My comrades-in-arms did not know the difference between a Duke and an Earl, and a Baronet might have been a man from Mars so far as they were concerned. Courtesy titles, borne by the offspring of peers – the eldest son before he inherits, and younger sons and daughters – were double-Dutch. That such high and low titles were generally bestowed for signal services to the nation – a war won, for example – crossed nobody's mind. The consensus was that toffs had got where they were by graft, that they were nothing special, were snooty bastards, and deserved to have their noses rubbed in the dust. Needless to say, in passing, that such views were broadcast in particular by the most upwardly mobile of radicals, who were impatient to bag the seats of power from which toffs had been ousted. As a result of my experience of the theoretical hostility to people like myself, even though in practice I never had any difficulty in crossing the class divide, I realised at the earliest stage of my literary career that I must not allow my writing to be judged by my breeding.

The social setting of *Morning* is privileged, I agree, but all the action revolves round a boy of six, seven or eight years of age, and his experience, as a kind critic was later to write, was universal. My intention had never been to describe a toff's world – indeed, I was already fairly sure that I would never be able to utilise aristocratic subject matter, which with few exceptions has been the province of the great middle class writers, Trollope, Evelyn Waugh – I was too close to it, and did not regard it romantically. The very last thing I wanted was to be revealed by my publisher as it were in the altogether, complete with my courtesy prefix, The Honourable – a gift to sneerers – and so answered Jock's query about autobiography with a sharpish negative.

The extra half of a reason that disappointed me in Jock was his stubborn worry as to which shelf in bookshops *Morning* would be consigned, the overcrowded one for fiction or the more *recherché* one for factual records that sell better in our dark age of art.

I reveal the guilty secret of yesteryear because I owe my extraordinary windfall, the subsequent parts of this volume, to the Westmorland connection; also because, with so many books to my name and other literary qualifications, I hope I can now proudly claim to be nothing but a writer.

Of course Jock was aware of my lineage, and he as it were provided the overture to later events.

The geography of the Murray headquarters at 50 Albemarle Street was a waiting room on the ground floor, and on the first floor Jock's office at the back of the house and a larger room at the front. In that elegant front room an elderly gent of military bearing attended to mysterious activities. Between these two rooms was a landing or lobby lined with books – John Murray publications – where tea with Madeira cake was served round about four o'clock.

I often partook of these refreshments. Jock and I would be joined by the old boy from across the way who spoke to me benevolently. He was Jock's relation near or far, and a full-blooded Murray whereas Jock had been a Grey and assumed the Murray surname when he became the heir to the business. One afternoon I was shown into the front room and forcibly reminded that Lord Byron had been a Murray author. As I recall, there were glass cases showing letters in Byron's hand and an array of memorabilia.

Other writers dropped in for tea at Murray's – Freya Stark, Peter Quennell, Paddy Leigh-Fermor – and the conversation nearly always reverted to Byron. Occasionally a book was launched with a cocktail party in Albemarle Street, and again the guests gravitated to the room on the first floor which served almost as a Byron museum. I was not especially interested, although an admirer of Byron's shorter poems – I had not read the longer ones. But after some talk of Byron, Jock put another question to me, a safely neutral question.

'By the way,' he asked, 'you don't happen to have a copy of Byron's *Memoirs* amongst your family papers, do you?'

What did he mean?

He enlightened me. Towards the end of his short life Byron wrote his *Memoirs*. He sent a copy back from Italy to the John Murray who published him – the courier was Thomas Moore. Murray and Moore read the manuscript and then solemnly, because it was so scandalous, burned it. The shameful act was perpetrated in the extant fireplace in the front room.

Jock continued: 'The only copy of the *Memoirs* not accounted for was lent to a Lady Westmorland, and has never come to light. You haven't seen it lying about somewhere at home, I suppose? Have a look! But don't look for a bulky pile of paper with "*Memoirs* by Byron" written in large letters on the top sheet. It must have been hot stuff, even before my predecessor put a match to it, and where you might find it is in a tome entitled *Household Accounts* or *Inventory*. The lady would have hidden it in the first instance, and when Byron died could not return it to him or let anyone else know she'd been reading a bawdy book. She might not have dared to destroy it – Byron was so famous, and his writings were so valuable – but just put it in one of those "safe places" where we lose things and forget them. It might turn up – you never know! And your family would profit enormously if it did.'

This snatch of conversation made not much of a dent on me. My lack of interest extended to my family history and even to filthy lucre – I was young and ignorant. Jock spoke to me on another occasion about Byron: he told me in conspiratorial accents that smoke in summer had been issuing from one of old Lady Wentworth's chimneys and that it was feared she too had been burning the Byron papers she had inherited. Lady Wentworth of Crabbet Park in Sussex was the famous breeder of Arab horses and a descendant of the poet. What did catch my attention briefly was the revelation that Jock was somehow keeping Lady Wentworth's home under surveillance. Otherwise, throughout this period of the publication of my first book and then my second, the only writer whose vicissitudes preoccupied me was myself.

One day I did mention the matter to my brother David. He was the new Lord Westmorland, the 15th, following our father's death, and was working hard to support his growing family. He was more uninterested than I had been, he was dismissive of the whole fairy tale. He had particular cause to be sceptical that anything of value was not popped by our grandfather, the last owner of the stately family pile, Apethorpe in Northamptonshire. Our grandfather came to financial grief at the turn of the nineteenth century either through the extravagance of his wife, or, more likely, by not collecting the rents of his tenant farmers who had been hit hard by the Repeal of the Corn Laws. I like to think it was the latter, that he had been generous as well as foolish. His or his agents' remedy to stave off bankruptcy was to sell his home, its contents, his land and estate, and virtually disinherit his children. It was a strange saga, a not particularly rakish rake's almost instantaneous progress from feast to famine, and the dispersal of centuries' accumulation of goods. David, his grandson, my brother, was heir to no pictures or furniture to speak of, and money likewise. I agreed with him that a literary goldmine could not credibly have been overlooked by a team of people scraping the bottom of every available barrel.

If by any outside chance the *Memoirs* existed in the keeping of the family, he remarked, it would be with the Westmorland Archive in the Northampton Records Office. What Archive, I asked. Oh – stuff placed there on permanent loan by our grandfather – deeds and things – he himself had never set eyes on them, but our solicitor had a list that I was welcome to ask to see. Was the stuff valuable? David did not know, but was intending to get a valuation and to sell if it would bring in a bob or two.

We dropped the subject. David was too busy to bother, and I decided it was all a red herring.

Inevitably I had to seek our solicitor's advice a few years later, and remembered that list. Was it available? Could I have a peep? The quarto pages handed over were more numerous than I expected and less comprehensible. Several entries were in Latin, others referred to persons and houses with names that rang no bells for me. One intriguing reference was to a document detailing the removal of the Westmorland caravanserai from one part of the country to another in the seventeenth century, the accommodation required along the way, the bookings of horses and meals, and the security arrangements. And the starred entry was an account book relating to the Battle of Agincourt. But nothing that could be the *Memoirs* sprang out, I could detect nothing promising or coded, and left it at that.

Again time passed. A friend of mine began to study Byron's work, and I informed him of my family's alleged connection. He persuaded me to fix up a visit to the Northampton Records Office, where we spent a pleasant day and were amused by an ante-diluvian recipe for roast chicken that gave instructions about the bird's diet from egg to oven. But otherwise we drew a blank.

My Westmorland grandfather, the one who sold Apethorpe and pretty well everything else he could lay his hands on, married twice. His first wife was Sybil St Clair-Erskine, daughter of the Earl of Rosslyn, whose family was renowned for its irresistible charm and its waywardness. Sybil was popular, and made her contribution to the ruin of her husband by buying flowers in Mayfair to fill her enormous house in Northants. She bore four children, the eldest being my father, and died of a combination of drink, drugs and lovers.

My grandfather then swung in the opposite matrimonial direction and married the daughter of a vicar, Catherine Geale. She outlived him by many years, and once, as Catherine Countess of Westmorland, wrote me a letter. She had heard that I was trying to become a writer, and offered to introduce me to a friendly scribe with experience who would 'teach me the tricks of the trade'. I was less tolerant in those days than I trust I am now, and wrote back to say that I intended to write in a manner exclusive of 'tricks', straightforwardly and adhering to the truth.

Our correspondence ended there, not surprisingly, and in the fullness of time Catherine died. We never met, but my letter, not hers, rankled, and I wished I had told her how sorry I was to have snubbed her good intention.

The sequel to the above could be compared to coals of fire on my head.

It was a letter from S— Bank, where blue blood has mingled with the purple of commerce immemorially. It was apologetic, a grovel of a dignified kind, and stated that the bank held in its vaults a small tin container belonging to me.

I had never banked at S—, and read on with surprise and mounting interest.

The container apparently had my name on it in the writing of Catherine Westmorland. There was a sheet of torn writing paper attached, on which she had written my name and signed her own. The letter from S— explained that they had been bankers to many of my forebears and particularly to my grandfather and his second Countess, that there had been an oversight on the part of her ladyship's executors and unfortunately the bank had omitted to correct it. The container had been stored in the bank in the mid-nineteenth century, it seemed, probably by my great-grandfather; possibly my grandfather was unaware of its existence; and Catherine, who inherited the residue of his estate, must have consigned it to me soon after I was born.

The bank's supposition was that she had altogether forgotten it, and ascribed its own forgetfulness to two wars, losses of paperwork due to enemy action, relocation and changes of staff. By way of reparation it offered to deliver the container to my Sussex home.

It arrived. The bank's description of the container was understated. It measured approximately eighteen inches by eight, had a coved or semi-circular lid, and was bound with strips of wood – they even followed the curves of the lid. If it was made of tin, the tin was infinitely superior to the tin of the cans that litter our landscape – much thicker. And it had an intricate key glued to its back, and hinged brass carrying-handles at each side. The weight of this luxury object also augured well.

I succeeded in chipping the key free and melting the glue that stuck to it. I turned the key in the lock with ease and lifted the lid. Beneath layers of yellow paper was a set of silver coffee cups and saucers.

I was disappointed, although Byron and his *Memoirs* were not in the forefront of my mind. I could not associate his surely indelicate writings with the daughter of a vicar. Bits of silver were all very well, I was not really *blasé*, but nor was I a coffee drinker or keen to polish silver. My first idea was that I would follow Grandfather's example and pop them.

Luckily they were in a good state and shiny because each cup and each saucer was wrapped in black tissue paper, as household hints prescribe. A second layer of wrapping were the yellow sheets already mentioned, which lined the bottom of the interior of the container and had acted as padding over the contents.

I had thrown these sheets, crumpled and uncrumpled, aside, on to the floor. Picking them up with the idea of consigning them to a waste paper basket, I noticed writing – they had handwriting back and front, faded but legible with difficulty. I straightened them out and shuffled them and to my astonishment on one memorable page read: George Gordon, 6th Lord Byron, and above a single word, *Diary*.

I did not believe it. My heart beat worryingly fast and hard, but I refused to believe that I was actually in possession of the copy of the *Memoirs* not burned by Moore and Murray.

I reassembled the sheets of paper in their numbered order. The letter to me from S— is dated 2001, August, so six months have elapsed between then and now, February 2002; and my work during those months has been almost exclusively putting two hundred and forty-three pages of *Diary* in sequence, deciphering the text, trying to make sense of what it was and might be, also of its arrival on my doorstep, and finally deciding how to deal with it. And I must confess that my initial surge of excitement was temporary, and replaced by successive stages of puzzlement, uncertainty, impatience, resentment, feelings that I was wasting my time and the conviction that I could never be repaid for wrestling with all the problems foisted upon me.

A solution to one of the problems occurred to me in the early days. The container, which is better described as a casket, belonged not to me but to another Julian Fane, the Victorian diplomat and poet. I must explain that my name, Christian and surname together, recurs throughout our family history – as I write, there are three more Julian Fanes knocking about: the farming Julian Fane of Fulbeck in Lincolnshire has difficulty in convincing the Inland Revenue that he is not writing books on the side. My poetic great-great-uncle is remembered nowadays, if at all, for having been the father of Etty Desborough and the grandfather of her son, another better poet, Julian Grenfell, who wrote the most heroic verses of World War I, *Into Battle*. That Julian Fane of yesteryear even looked Byronic and dressed Byronically – a painting of him in my home corroborated that he was meant to be the recipient of the manuscript.

But more information was winkled out of S— Bank: it had a record of the casket in its safe keeping in the 1920s, near the year of my birth, 1927. Catherine could have given it to me, through the agency of a scrap of paper, by way of a christening present. That she ever read the *Diary* is difficult to credit, and would the vicar's daughter have given such a book to a baby? The possibility that she merely redirected a family heirloom from one Julian Fane to another, myself, was a reasonable conjecture. Still, how the *Diary* became the property of the Westmorlands was a different question.

Clearly I would have to venture deeper into the maze of family history.

The 10th Earl of Westmorland was born in 1759 and died in 1841. His second wife, whom he married in 1800, was Emily Saunders, a doctor's daughter. Emily outlived her husband by sixteen years, and died in 1857.

How were Emily Westmorland and Byron acquainted?

I own a copy of Byron's letters, edited by Leslie Marchand and published by John Murray – personally by my sometime publisher Jock – in twelve volumes. In Volume 3, a letter from Byron dated June 1813 to Lady Westmorland apologises for 'affronts I did not offer and offences I do not understand'. Apparently Emily's step-daughter, Lady Jersey, had given a party attended by Lady Caroline Lamb, who walked out after declining to be introduced to Byron because 'there were too many women about him'; and Caroline complained to her hostess who complained to her step-mother, who wrote to Byron, accusing him of bad behaviour. The end of which story was no doubt Byron's additional apology to Caro followed by her leap into his bed – thus the world wags.

Byron comments on this storm in a society teacup in a letter to Lady Melbourne, mother-in-law of Caroline Lamb: 'Your plague and mine [B's reference to Caroline] has been in "excellent

17

fooling" … I wish she would not call in the aid of so many compassionate Countesses – there is Ly W[estmorland] (with a tongue too) conceives me to be the greatest Barbarian since the days of Bacchus and Ariadne…'

In 1814 Byron, in another letter to Lady Melbourne, refers to Lady W: '… The abominable stories they circulate about Lady Wd of which I can say no more … why, the woman is a fright – which after all is another reason for not believing [them].'

In 1817, Byron writes to Hobhouse from Venice and perhaps sheds light on these 'stories'. He hopes that 'Dr Polidori, a successful young person in the drug line,' who has been the death of Lord Guilford, Mr Horner and Mr Hope's son, will have had better luck with 'Lady Westmorland's C…s – which is supposed to be of the longest…' In the same letter Byron refers to 'the Sapphic Westmorland'.

Was lesbianism what was 'abominable' in the gossip about Lady W? Yet if she was a lesbian, Dr Polidori was bound to be unlucky. And a further reference to Dr Polidori piles contradiction on confusion.

From Venice, still in 1817, Byron wrote to John Murray: 'Talking of Doctors reminds me once more to recommend to you one who will not recommend himself, the Doctor Polidori… If you have any sick relation – I would advise his advice – all the patients he had in Italy are dead – Mr Hope's son – Mr Horner – & Lord Guilford – whom he embowelled with great success at Pisa. – The present Lord Guilford – who was the Charlatan Frederic North & the Lady Westmorland – will I hope do something for him – it is a pity the last don't keep him – I think he would suit her – he is a very well looking man – and it would not be to her discredit.'

Byron made a final epistolary reference to my relation by marriage in a letter to Scrope Davies, again in 1817 – or was he making a joke?

He runs through the casualties of Dr Polidori's medical attention, adding '45 paupers in Pisa' to the trio of Ld Guilford, Mr Horner and Mr Hope's son, and under the italicised title 'wounded' writes: 'Lady Westmorland – incurable – her disease not defined.'

The disease cannot have been completely incurable, since her ladyship did not die for forty more years.

In view of these cynical and humorous quotations, where on earth did Jock Murray get the idea that Byron had entrusted one of two or maybe three copies of his *Memoirs* to Emily Westmorland? Byron's letters fill eleven full-length books plus an informative index, yet he deals with Lady W in brief references amounting to some one hundred and fifty words. They cannot have been friends, he mocked her, there is no evidence of her literary interests, he wrote to her in person once; yet according to Jock, in the six years between the completion of his

Memoirs and his death, he told one of his intimates or correspondents that she was or had been in temporary possession of this treasure.

Artists are not careless. They may look bedraggled and smell like badgers, they may live in Bohemian squats, but, as a rule, they never forget the effusions of their art, and how well or badly people and critics react to them. Byron was not so cavalier with his work as with his women. He claimed to think his *Memoirs* could not be published in his lifetime; but writers have often yielded to requests to redefine the meaning of the word 'posthumous' – Chateaubriand spent many years giving readings from his *Mémoires d'outre tombe*. Byron submitted a copy of the *Memoirs* to his wife, asking her to delete anything she disliked or disapproved of – a careful gesture, although he should have known that she would decline to read it and beg him not to publish for the sake of their child Ada's future happiness. He showed it to Lady Holland, Hobhouse, Moore and Murray, and the latter paid two thousand guineas for it – circumstances reminiscent of the hopes of authors who have just finished a new work and wish it to reach the widest possible readership in the best possible shape.

Lady Westmorland does not figure in the bona fide list of readers of the *Memoirs,* nor, more significantly, did Byron reveal the slightest concern in respect of a copy of this libellous and immensely valuable document remaining in the hands of a society woman with a probably mischief-making tongue.

What then, if no linkage can be established between Lady W, Byron and his *Memoirs*, were the sheets of paper in the casket, and how did they get there?

Simply to hold them gave me an inkling of the passion of collectors for holograph material. They might have been touched and hallowed by the hand of genius. The writing slants forwards energetically, the strokes of the pen – quill or metal? – are heavy, and Byron's original punctuation, his characteristic rash of dashes, assaults the eye. Neither a line, nor an occasional circular spill of ink, seems to have been blotted. Perhaps I was the owner of a forgery, a nineteenth-century fake – counterfeiters getting on for two centuries ago were surely as crafty as the writer of *Hitler's Diary* which fooled *The Times* and succeeded in extracting money from Rupert Murdoch. Whoever the writer was, his fluency and confidence are reminders that it either was written, or was meant to have been, when Byron was young, not yet in his mid-thirties.

Legibility was another matter. A side-effect of Byron writing in a hurry was slow reading. Crossings-out and inserts had bewildering consequences. Some inserts were written vertically in margins. But after all John Murray learned to transcribe his hieroglyphics into English, and at last I was able to fill the gaps in my initial transcript and piece together the whole.

Belatedly, I saw the point that it was nothing like a proper diary or journal, nor did it resemble in any respect the book burned at 50

Albemarle Street and many years later described by Jock Murray. And common sense led me towards more realistic hypotheses. Possibly the notorious De Gibler, a counterfeiter on the lunatic fringe who assumed the alias Major George Gordon Byron, had played safe and split a legal hair by calling his forgery a *Diary* rather than the *Memoirs*, which was widely known not to exist. The alternative was that Byron himself, writing several years after his *Memoirs* came to nought, and recording the train of events that shunted him towards Missolonghi and unknowingly or knowingly to his death, decided to shun a disastrous title and settle for one he had already used to moderately good effect.

He wrote five conventional diaries in his lifetime. Some were published in versions edited and cut by Thomas Moore. There is no record of a sixth diary – mine.

In its last pages Byron puts forward reasons that reinforce and coincide with my own tentative resolution of the mystery of how it has ended up in my possession.

The first chapter of two was obviously unpublishable for ages after it was written. Lord Grey de Ruthyn, or his descendants, would have taken great exception to Byron's accusations. The same applies to his revelations in respect of the home life of the Joneses, and Harrow School might well have objected in days more straitlaced than ours.

The second chapter was even more indiscreet by nineteenth-century standards. Lady Caroline Lamb, who was saddened to see by accident the funeral cortège of Byron proceeding back to his family home, Newstead Abbey in Nottinghamshire, would have been shattered to read his comments on their love affair. She and her husband William Lamb, later Queen Victoria's Prime Minister Lord Melbourne, and the powerful older generation of their families, would have conspired together to censor all Byron's trenchant and ungrateful references to his former mistress. And the rest of Part Two would have made sickening reading for the Contessa Teresa Guiccioli, not to mention the Conte, or, for that matter, for the couple renamed with partial pity, Eve and Timothy.

The *Diary* was apparently written just before Byron left Italy to go to free Greece from its Turkish invaders. He might have sent it to Murray in accordance with previous practice – to his friend and factotum as well as his publisher. But he no doubt surmised that Murray, having seen the £2000 he paid for the *Memoirs* go up the Albemarle Street chimney in smoke, would try to recoup his loss by bringing out an eviscerated edition of this 'diary'. He was at least twice shy of letting Murray get his teeth into it, and was forced by considerations both artistic and financial to think of a better way. He had already given vast sums of money to the Greek cause, and was facing further appeals and expenses when he would be living in the country.

Plausibly, the scene was set for the Westmorlands to play their part in the comedy or tragedy.

I have explained that my family is 'old' in the sense that it dates back almost to the primeval slime. I exaggerate – unlike the Cecils, we own no family tree that traces our ancestry to Adam and Eve; nor am I boasting, for as a rule the oldest families survive by keeping the lowest possible profile, in other words by being unambitious, undistinguished, and usually uncouth backwoodsmen. An exception to that rule in our case was the 11th Earl, a general, an eminent diplomat, a fine musician, decorated for his services to many countries.

To put things into perspective historically: Emily Westmorland, Byron's acquaintance, died in 1857. John, the Earl referred to above, was her step-son, and died in 1859 – he and his step-mother were contemporaries. Whether or not they were on good terms, they both moved in high society, where the top secret is that there are no secrets.

Byron was not discreet, certainly not so discreet as to tell no one that he had dashed off a couple of autobiographical pieces; and he had friends, correspondents and servants, all of whom were interested for one reason or another in his writings. Word of the *Diary* was likely to have spread; and either in reply to curious questions, or voluntarily, Byron could have dropped hints that he was prepared to part with the manuscript on certain conditions in return for ready money.

The Westmorlands heard about it, I suggest. Emily might have told John, who had four sons, including my namesake, Julian Fane, the poet in the Byronic mould. The musical father and the literary son would have been wise to agree that the purchase of the *Diary* was a grand idea, since they would be supporting the arts represented by Byron, they could afford to accept the condition that the MS should be shielded from prying eyes for a long time, they were promised a solid capital gain when they were at last able to market it, and in view of the family's talent for survival they were confident that some future Fane would benefit from the investment.

Alas, two of John Westmorland's sons predeceased their father, and Julian Fane did not outlive him for long. And during such a plague of dying, successive and foolproof testamentary instructions would not necessarily have been issued.

In time John's widow, Priscilla, niece of the Iron Duke of Wellington, coming across the equivalent of a naughty book, even if she knew the author was Byron, wrapped it round a set of silver coffee cups, locked it away from prying eyes in a casket, and consigned it to storage in S— Bank – that is my imaginary scenario. I shall take it further: Priscilla was naturally disinclined to let her only daughter see it – she was mortified to find herself in charge of it, and may not even have listed it in her own will or posthumous wishes. The casket got itself forgotten, since I am afraid the 12th Earl of Westmorland was traditionally dim, the 13th, my grandfather, was as limited as his loss of the Westmorland fortune indicates, and the 14th, my father, had no grasp of business or practical matters.

The conclusion I had jumped to, that the casket might have belonged to the other Julian Fane, was not necessarily so wide of the mark. But the casket cannot have borne his name or any indication of whose property it was – the bankers at S— would have acted sooner if they had known who owned it. My guess is that my christening reminded Catherine Westmorland of something my grandfather had told her about a container, a box containing stuff said to be worth a pretty penny, that was somehow connected with his poetic great-uncle Julian and had been stowed away goodness knew where. She discovered that a likely sort of box existed in the bank, and bequeathed it to me on account of my name by means of a piece of paper that was easily damaged and overlooked.

I cannot vouch for the authenticity of the work that follows. I have consulted no literary expert as yet, nor have I paid for the services of science, for carbon dating and so on. I am neither an historian nor a pedant, and in this Explanation my chronology and other minutiae may well be imprecise. Therefore, so as not to be accused of a confidence trick, so as to mislead no one and risk nothing, I present my slim volume as a novella.

After much consultation, I decided to give readers exactly what I was given, in order to let them see for themselves and draw their own conclusions. Why should the scholars and scientists have all the fun of deciding whether the *Diary* is fact or fiction? I would remind amateurs that even in Byron's short adult life, say between the ages of seventeen and his death at thirty-six, forged letters in the likeness of his handwriting were being peddled and sold. His style was easy to copy: the semi-colloquial rush of his prose, the eccentric grammar and his individualistic dots and dashes, are all gifts to the forger. And I am afraid I cannot guarantee that no Lord Westmorland ever bought a pup.

Yet how tempting it is to suspend disbelief in the present instance! The forger seems to know more than he would or could have known: arguably, Byron was the writer. I was never able to understand why he sacrificed so much, the company of the beautiful and loving Teresa, the upkeep of his illustrious reputation, luxury, financial security, in order to strike something of a pose in a bespoke military uniform on an unhealthy shore of Greece: the *Diary* reveals that it was not only idealism which took him to Missolonghi.

Presumably, in due course, the clever people who can tell the difference between the real thing and a real sham will settle the matter one way or the other.

Meanwhile I have to decide how to bring the *Diary* to the attention of the public, bearing in mind that it could supersede thousands of biographies. Jock Murray presided over great advances in the study of Byron, man and poet, and perhaps his family firm deserves to be shown it. But when I was his author, and after he had told me about the burning of the *Memoirs* in the room beyond the landing where we drank tea and ate Madeira cake, I shared a humorous thought with another Murray author, John Betjeman. We both suspected that if the actual *Memoirs* should be found and entrusted to Jock, he too would decide they were unpublishable and burn them in the same infamous grate. We meant not that he was a prude or a vandal, but extremely cautious – we thought he would not wish to offend the descendants of those ladies whom Byron had obliged and those gentlemen he had cuckolded, or to raise doubts in respect of the blood in the veins of the upper crust.

John and I were probably wrong – it was a joke. Jock became less fussy about the tone of Murray[1] books as he grew older. Anyway, the *Diary* is pure and harmless in comparison with most modern books, and I expect Jock's professional successors are models of open-mindedness and integrity. Yet I wonder if they would care or

---

[1] In May 2002, John Murray (Publishers) Ltd was bought by Hodder Headline, a subsidiary of W.H. Smith. Murray's was founded in 1768, and its decline and fall is probably the last nail in the coffin of old-style publishing, which favoured quality rather than quantity, and tried to be polite to authors.

dare to publish me – or Byron – again. An alternative would be to do as Byron did in his youth – publish the *Diary* myself and keep it in my family for a little longer.

DIARY

by

George Gordon
6th Lord Byron

PART ONE

They called my father Mad Jack – he was as profligate as handsome – but he inherited the courage of his father, my grandfather, Admiral John, a Jack of another colour, Foulweather Jack. Energy to be good or bad – to be brave enough to face up to life – energy equals victory and lack of it defeat, nothing between. I am the son of my forefathers for better or worse.

My mother was Scottish – she embodied every Scottish fault. She was born thrifty and rich, and compounded that unfortunate combination by marrying my father – he spent her money and seared her parsimonious soul. Stubborn fidelity was her idea of matrimony – no surprise he felt compelled to spread his wings – Byrons are a race of exceptions to the British rule of hypocrisy. I did not know my father – was almost a fatherless babe – but understand how much he must have hated her and forgive him for leaving me to suffer the lashes of her knotted tongue.

We were poor in Aberdeen, a tragedy twice over – in that granite city, hearts seemed to partake of the character of its building materials. We lived in lodgings, were short of essentials, and did not mix with the generality – my mother was ashamed of her fallen state. – Her conversation was repeatedly to condemn my father to the fires of hell, hoping he was burning slowly – imagine how enjoyable for a boy not yet in his teens! She was angry to have had her money frittered on fun and games, she was furious to be a widow and to lack the financial attractions that might have trapped a second husband. Yet she was no fright to look at – had the fresh complexion of Scots which derives from their confidence that they are never wrong – she was a healthy female not altogether beyond the pale of male interest – and she would not lift her skirt a single inch to remedy her situation – she thought she was too important to have her bacon saved by an Aberdonian.

Children love their mothers – they prefer a cruel mother to none – and I was no exception – hugged her the harder if I was given leave to do so – lisped the word dearest in the accepted style – questioned nothing while I learned to name my emotions. But at five or six I became aware of a difference between truth and a lie, and was embarrassed to be asked by strangers in the street and shops, 'Ye're awful fond of that mother of yours, a'nt you, laddie?' I could only agree with fingers crossed. It was a shortish step from there to my active and conscious dislike of my parent, and my resentment that I should have any of her blood in my veins – or, in more sophisticated terms, that I should be bound to her by mercenary considerations and by the unsheddable umbilical connection until death parted us.

Our cohabitation while I proceeded from

eight to nine, ten and eleven years of age is a ghastly remembrance. We were too physically close for comfort in our two and a half rooms to lodge in – I had outgrown them as well. Open warfare was declared between us when I commanded her not to berate my poor father. Who's telling me to shut my mouth? – that was her response. I am, said I, and I shall strike you now or when I am bigger if you do not stop forthwith. She demurred, she dared to slap my face – Scots are not amenable to orders – but I was as good as my word and blacked her eye. That settled it for the moment – but her new respect for me was temporary – and although I had quelled her I had done it by means of anger and effort, whereas her violence was characteristic and cost her nothing – therefore she won future battles because I was reluctant to expend my vitality and nervous resources on her unworthiness.

The melancholy strain in my work – loathed by reviewers, not by readers – doubtless dates back to the three or four years in question. I was locked up with a woman I detested and the sentence had no end in view. I was chained to my enemy, her shrewishness rankles yet – her discovery of faults in every word I spoke, every essay I scrawled, in my attire, in my person. She was careful not to assault me again, threaten me tho' she did, but her aggression was nonetheless wicked for being verbal. Needless to say that when she had exhausted her synonyms for dunce and devil's spawn, she had recourse to criticism of the misshapen foot she and my father between them had visited upon me. She would bewail its ugliness, call me cripple, expatiate on the cost of a shoe to cover it up, foretell that no woman would ever bear to look at it or at me – in all her life she never ceased to make mistakes. My feelings could still be hurt – I had not the philosophy to laugh at her in my turn – and sadness prevailed as the prospect of an unchangeable future overhung my present. Later, to the surprise of the companions of my manhood, melancholy was seen not to be an obvious part of my make-up – it had gone underground and slipped out and into my verses without my connivance – that is my interpretation of the scarring of my early youth on my temperament.

But fate allowed me to rise from the ashes of my start in life. I can hardly call the workings of a social system dating back to the dawn of time a miracle – it was a preordained accident of my breeding – yet to my twelve years of ignorance it had a whiff of divine intervention. In my inmost heart I sensed it might have been an equivalent of the Annunciation – but I have no desire to blaspheme.

My reference is to my elevation to the peerage – my becoming from one minute to the next the superior of my mother – and the rosy fingers of light that stole across the view of my prospects.

It was not expected – it should have been but was not – my mother either did not understand the chance for me in the offing, or else did not make clear that one day I would be able to lord it over her – on the other hand, to be fairer to her than she ever was, the failing might have been on my side. The gentleman who was my benefactor in the end – his end – was remote, unknown, grand beyond the range of my experience, and took no interest in a great-nephew who was paying the price of the sins of his father. Lordship was a dream for me long after I was called My Lord, and I have little recollection of the joyous occasion of my great-uncle's funeral or the honeyed words that went over my head in the chambers of solicitors. My sympathy for the downtrodden is the consequence of my luck in discovering I was no longer poor, weak, dependent, hopeless – in my inheritance of such a great relief – and of the pain of knowing of the bad luck, the lack of luck like mine, of the many.

I was rich *in principle*, but being so was costly even to the point of ruination – that was the reverse of the glad tidings that had been announced. My inheritance was not only the 6th Lordship of Byron and the fine estate of Newstead Abbey, granted to my forebears by King Henry VIII, but also the news that the lordly cupboard was bare, Newstead was saddled with debt, and money in esoteric accounts and funds would not be released to me until the lawyers saw fit – sometime never, no doubting. Solicitors! – a word to instil terror in the bravest heart, to cast a blight at least on the bright shoots of the spring time of everyman! Oh the humming and hawing of those dusty men in their dusty chambers – what insoluble problems they unearthed touching the future state and conditions of life of the boy peer who could not be dragged up in a slum street in Aberdeen – who should not rot in lodgings with an unmaternal mother until he could earn his daily bread – who ought to be protected from the pauperism and wretchedness reserved for commoners!

The arguments were lost on me – I quote the snobbish battle cries of my mother – and breathed more freely when a settlement of sorts was arrived at – the relevant part of which for myself was that change would occur despite my worst prognostications, and I would go to school, where my mother would not be in attendance.

The engine of this true beginning of my existence, freed from bondage, were four letters of the alphabet to which I had already been introduced and with which I was to become dreadfully familiar – the letters are d, e, b, t. At a later stage than the point in my story already reached, when large sums of money had been promised me but were not received – when promises of wealth had been invariably broken – I adopted the solution worked out for my salvation by solicitors, and borrowed money against my expectations and the bricks and mortar of my home. I followed the well-trodden path to the premises of the Tribe of Levi, retraced my steps light-heartedly, and smiled less often for ever after – usury was the second rack that has tortured me. Yes, I was better for the money borrowed to maintain my dignity and send me to school, happier at Cambridge to entertain my friends with generous hospitality than to sit and study by a low fire behind a locked door, fortunate to afford the leisure to respond to my vocation and win renown with my pen – but how high the price, what wakings to the recollection that my money was not my own and I owed far more than I could repay! My emancipation was long in coming – in a way it was bought with my exile from my country and my having no further need of beloved Newstead, from which unwarranted persecution banished me, over the sale of which I shed my tears, but where I will lay my bones and find my peace.

The school I was sent to was Harrow, Harrow on the Hill, overlooking London, and there I met gentlemen of my standing and formed friendships that defined my mind – masters were less influential than boys – and reading taught me what I could not learn in class. The Rubicon of puberty was crossed in my sleep, a symbolical comment by nature on the confusion and bewilderment of our biographies – for on one side of the Rubicon we know nothing of the world, literally nothing, and on the other we know everything save how to adapt our knowledge to save our souls – we sleep, we sleepwalk, throughout our journey – or do I speak only for myself? The most educative of all schools I now metaphorically attended, the school of love. I formed the highest regard for a cousin of mine – she was my angel, perfectly pure and high above me – and repelled lusty images and would not allow my eyes to wander or curiosity to inflame my baser instincts. My first poems were declarations of love – all poetry may be outpourings either for love or against it – and I revelled and despaired along with the rest and best of men.

Newstead was let – I had spent time under its roof and absorbed new feelings for my family and a strong attachment to its cradle and its hearth – I revelled in my ownership of the place, even while I shared it with my mother. But the devil was driving, and lawyers told me needs must – I must leave it for lucre, rent it out to keep pace with my indebtedness, tho' not to pay my debts – that paradise of indemnification lay over the horizon and out of sight. My tenant was Lord Grey de Ruthyn, scion of lineage older than mine, gentleman by birth at any rate, and not far beyond my own age – the few years that make so great a difference in the days of youth. – I met him – we were introduced – he shook my hand warmly and spouted that I would be his friend as well as his landlord – I reciprocated to the best of my manners and inclinations – and allowed him to take possession of my home.

He then invited me to stay. I was unwilling, but my mother would have me go – she was bowled over by Lord Grey who had kissed *her* hand and paid her fulsome compliments – she persuaded me on the grounds that I should inspect my property and see that it suffered no harm. The story of my visit has not been told – under the greatest provocation from my inquisitive parent I vowed never to tell it – I meant not to tell her, and have it cried from the rooftops – but the Lordling has met his Maker by now and, tho' I would not damage his child, I have no scruples in putting a brief account of it on paper which will not be read until interested parties will either have reached an age of discretion or be under the sod.

I went to Nottinghamshire, to Newstead. Lord Grey had no other company in the house. His eyeing of me stirred memories of older boys when I was first at school, but I was still so green in such affairs that I remained unsure of the meaning of the Harrovian looks I had been treated to, and could not believe that a peer of the realm could possibly sink to entertain thoughts resembling those rude ones – I phrase it politely. Neighbours were at supper on the first night – and the table was not short of liquid sustenance – as soon as we were alone Lord Grey, drunk or feigning drunkenness, begged me to help him upstairs and put him to bed. I did the first task, but declined the second, retired to my room, and was interrupted in my reading by the peer in his nightshirt stumbling in and suggesting a pillow fight – I sent him packing, and wondered when I could escape without forming a judgment or making a scene.

The next morning he behaved as if oblivious of the night's events – but as the day wore on his gestures grew more affectionate – when I recoiled he resorted to the justification of his seniority, and seemed to accuse me of harbouring vulgar suspicions. He talked much of his aristocratic rights and privileges, and occasionally condescended to switch from the first person singular to the first person plural. He was a vain fop, and wore shoes with high heels in the country so that he could look closer into my eyes or look down his nose at me. Night fell, and I had been patted enough to make me into butter – we again retired – and this time my visitor revealed his intentions by the tent-like shape of his nightshirt. 'Sir,' said I in reproachful tones – 'Dearest,' said he in reply – I pushed him towards the door – he resisted and there was a tussle which ended through no fault of mine in his thanking me – I got rid of him without further difficulty, and decided to depart post-haste and not to bother to spare his feelings.

He returned to my room in the following dawn – I called him a blackguard and told him that I refused to submit to any more indignities – he cried and begged for my mercy – undressed and implored me to do the same – I summoned the servants, and was soon travelling back to the haven of my mother's love and sympathy.

She cursed me. She swore at me for not revealing why I had chosen to offend my admirable host, a gentleman of distinction if ever there was one, who in her firm opinion was incapable of an ignoble action. She insisted first on my immediate return to Newstead, secondly on composing a letter of abject apologies and lies which I would sign and send to Lord Grey, lastly, as always, she called me a brute, a bear, too proud to live, too ugly to gain acceptance in polite society, as ugly as my foot, a cripple in body and character. By good luck more than good management I was required at Harrow, and extracted myself from the claws of the unnatural woman who my father Jack must indeed have been mad to marry and impregnate.

Neither a Puritan nor a hypocrite am I. – Yet there was – there is, I would claim – a certain purity inseparable from youth, from the time before corruption has begun to gnaw at us and spread its unstoppable infection. My love of my love, of idealised womanhood in general, of imaginary gentle creatures who must exist and be the antithesis of my mother – of the she who would hold my heart in her soft hands for ever and understand me – that precious image was defaced and soiled by His Lordship of Grey. He called me dearest and dared to speak to me of the emotion towards which I aspired – my Holy Grail was spat upon – he cut me to the quick with his weapon. Could love be anything like that of which he spoke? Could it be force and violence? Unanswered questions – questions I was ashamed to put to anyone else – which I was too serious to laugh at and dismiss – tho' in time I saw the humorous aspect of one peer fighting to repel the advances of another.

As for hypocrisy, I will acknowledge that I have not been above Platonism – in my time at

Cambridge I cared for a sweet uneducated boy, and was myself blackguarded for misleading him into unnatural practices, which was never true – I did him no damage, on my honour. I love beauty, I have searched for and loved it throughout my life, no more and no less – the ugliness of the behaviour of my tenant, and the desires he exhibited, grated against my innocence and were not to my taste. Perverse I will not call these desires – I have had trouble with that adjective in relation to my sister Augusta, my half-sister, as the whole world knows – which was again a misjudgment. The truth of the matter, experience would agree, is that love between a man and a woman bleaches every *sin* of the flesh – the deeper the love the more it cleanses – all is natural in those extremes of intimacy.

I risk another dose of the pillory for refusing to tell lies – that is the law in England – only liars escape punishment – inconsistency is the essence of English respectability. – In which case I have not been respectable, unlike Lord Grey of Ruthyn. He married and produced a daughter – a tremendous effort on his part considering his excitement of which I had been the cause – a nice example of hypocrisy, I would hazard a guess – but paternity was too much for him, he expired shortly after doing the *natural* thing.

The cousin[1] I loved was far away, and I was

---

[1] Her name was Mary Chaworth.

growing toward adulthood – these circumstances would have to be called temporary. The possibility that Lord Grey had stimulated me, if in a different direction from that which he had pointed at, I will not confirm but cannot deny. The connection between love and sexuality was established – demonstrated to a certain extent – and a novel lack of chastity disturbed my romantic reveries. Could-it-be took over from surely-not in my imagination, and restlessness undermined my concentration.

Study was problematic, studiousness eluded me, bad marks followed, and classes led to clashes with tutors and teachers. A tutor called Jones began to torment me – I took the view that he was insolent and not addressing me with the respect to which my position entitled me, while he indicated that he thought me arrogant and deserved to have my wings clipped before I flew beyond his range. – He seemed antediluvian to me but cannot have been more than in his forties, and I fancied he was a typical product of Harrow's county, Middlesex, for he was of middling height, middling spare of figure, middling bald, and middling *chalky*. He had a wide thin-lipped mouth, brown teeth, and a sarcastic manner – he smiled when he hurt his pupils verbally – he would not have ventured on violence for he was dealing with large strong boys who would not have brooked it. – He was a nobody in the street, an unnoticeable skulking sort, scuttling by with downcast eyes and a bag of books – but a tyrant in class, enjoying his hour of power, exercising his momentary authority, and ridiculing our faults and errors. His Christian name was Theodore, which means Gift of God, but none could believe the Almighty had done more than to give him away and be shot of him as soon as possible.

Theodore Jones displeased me, and I was never one to swallow my displeasure, as Scotch reviewers found out when I stood up for English bards, myself not least. His sarcasm was of the common or garden variety, and has been resorted to by schoolmasters throughout the history of education. Would Lord Byron be minded to tell us – can His Lordship be bothered to give us the information – will His Lordship be so good as to – may I thank the noble lord on behalf of the class for shedding light on our cultural darkness? – thus he taunted and discouraged. He gave me extra essays to write on particularly inspiring subjects – for examples The Produce of Holland or The Trade of the Farrier – as a rule I would bring them to the class after the one on which I had been awarded punishment for not having listened spellbound to his disquisitions – but then he shortened the time allowed me to write punitive lines and on a memorable occasion demanded that I deliver the work to the house he occupied.

The season was late summer – dusk was falling on a balmy day – I was late on account of conflict between my essay and my cricket – and had walked fast to the Jones' residence, a cottage barely above the dignity of an artisan, and pulled the bell.

Not Jones but a woman of stature and some grace, smiling her welcome, opened the door. I offered her the papers, after a second's hesitation she insisted on my coming indoors – she said I needed a *breather*. She repeated my name as if with some satisfaction – Lord Byron, goodness me! – and I, not concluding instantly that she could be the wife of the hominoid Jones, begged for details of her identity.

She said she was Mrs Jones. I must have displayed surprise and scepticism, since she was so superior to her Mister, and she turned away in such a manner as seemed to me to denote agreement, regret and resignation. I entered her abode, which hardly merits the epithet humble – a narrow passage, steep stairs rising, parlour to left, dining-room to right, all smelling of wax polish and poverty – and was ushered into her plushy parlour. I asked for the schoolmaster – I had a packet to hand to him – and she told me he was absent, had been called away on some urgent business, and had instructed her to accept the item. When she held it she glanced at the top page and read out the title written there, *The Purpose of Education*, and inquired with a smile *Were you inspired by the subject, sir?* I explained that it was given me – that title – not for the purpose of pleasure, more for pain or penalty. Why and wherefore, she wanted to know – because, I replied, I had not attended to her husband's words of wisdom as I should have done. She laughed, we laughed – her laughter sympathetic and conspiratorial – I realised afterwards that she too was apt to be inattentive.

I then thanked her and bade her goodbye, but she delayed my going by asking if I would come to tea on a day in no way penal, would I be allowed, was it a done thing? I was 'twixt Scylla and Charybdis, not wanting to take tea in the company of Jones, who would poison it for me, and not on principle able to resist a challenge of any description – besides I had developed a liking and even a bond with the lady. I mumbled yes – which was part of the answer – and retreated and took my leave.

It was nothing, except gossip to share with my cronies – that desiccated Jones had a Missis who was good-looking and juicy enough for four times the man she had wed. It was more a mystery than anything else, for I did not yet know that there is no accounting for the preferences of females, who have a tendency to turn up their noses at Apollo and pine for a weakling short of all recognisable attractions. The incident would have been forgotten if Jones had not continually and unintentionally reminded me of his wife.

An invitation to tea arrived – she had chosen a half-holiday when I would be free, that is without an easy excuse for refusing. I dreaded it – Jones in class equalled satiety – I was disinclined to stoop to friendship with him – even his wife would not dilute his personality to a digestible level. But I trooped along, and she alone admitted me – Jones was absent throughout, no explanation vouchsafed. We ate tea in the parlour – servants not visible either – and from a shy start she prompted me to talk – talk even of my private poetic hopes and, inevitably, say much that I was sorry for afterwards – she showed interest, she flattered and led me on, and I cannot pretend that I was averse to it. Our parting verged on the affectionate – she patted my hand instead of shaking it – and wondered if I would return on another occasion – to which my response was affirmative – and she let me out, again with momentary hesitation on the doorstep, during which she scanned the street to ascertain that we were not spied upon – but I did not know the reason why until later.

I must have been made for adultery, my history proves it, for, although nothing more passed between Mrs Jones and myself than I have faith-fully recorded, I made a point of not speaking to Jones of my tea party with his wife, and noted that Jones did not speak of it to me, con-cluding that he might not have been informed of its occurrence. Less of an ignoramus would have realised that he was being lured into the perilous terrain of secrets, and that what I regarded as tea and compensation for Jones bullying me to produce essays on dreary sub-jects, Mrs Jones saw in a different light, fraught with incipient emotion and illegal excitement.

But my knuckle-headedness has excuses. I was in my seventeenth year, and retarded doubtless

by lack of proper schooling and scant comrade-
ship with other boys until I was thirteen. I had
not fully adjusted to my dramatic changes of
fortune and masculinity, and had the merest
inkling of the ways of the world – my head was
in the clouds, amidst skies of purest blue for all
the storm stirred up by Lord Grey. And I was
confronted by a situation composed of unlikely
ingredients – a woman I thought of as old, wife
of a schoolmaster with an antipathy to me, a
couple respectable by definition, whose earnings
were dependent on their respectability, and an
acquaintanceship that surely breached the strict
code of conduct governing all concerned in the
running of a famous public school. Moreover, I
have to add, being the son of my mother, that
there was a social chasm separating the potential
parties to further involvement.

Another invitation arrived. It was again to tea,
and I accepted it more willingly than before.
The circumstances were the same, the conversation included a different story, hers rather than
mine. Yet again I was flattered both by her calling me Poet and by the receipt of confidences.
She had married too young – her matrimonial
hopes had not been fulfilled – she had not been
blessed with children – she was often lonely. She
yearned for friendship and wished to encourage
and help me with my versifying – she lived for
poetry and believed writing it to be the highest
of all occupations for a gentleman – would I
honour her with permission to read something
of mine that sprung from the heart? – not

stupid old essays. Certainly, said I – I would push a package of poems through her letter-box without delay. No, said she, nothing like that, I must bring the poetry and give it into her hand – there must be no premature publicity, and she was afraid that her husband, who detested poetry, might exert a baleful influence on the sensitive processes of creation.

Still I smelt no rat – even her disloyalty to her spouse for the sake of loyalty to me passed me by. Like a good dog, I answered to her whistle, and when the only hunger I was aware of had been satisfied with toast and buns we sat close on her sofa, she leaning against me to read over my shoulder. She was complimentary – my temperature was raised by her compliments – and, briefly, in the space of one of those seconds on which histories hinge, I saw her and metaphorically felt her in a different way. – Breath was to blame – and why not? – breathing gives us life and not breathing kills us – she breathed close to my ear abnormally, shallowly, and I began to mimic her – I was lured into the outer circle of the sexual playground by our rhythmic inhaling. There was no advantage taken, but in a sort of suspension of activity I was conscious as never before of her womanliness, long hair, complexion, teeth, hands, body heat and fragrance – with apologies, the hackneyed description of arousal. Did she feel the same? No, impossible, I had mistook, I blushed with embarrassment to be entertaining squalid physical symptoms within inches of her wifehood and kindness.

She stood up abruptly – I was afraid she had detected my condition and was about to rebuke me – and I glanced at her apologetically. She was flushed, and she avoided my eyes – we avoided each other's – and she said perhaps I should go – words open to sexual interpretations. I gathered my papers together – she said I was not to leave them lying about – and made haste to depart, mumbling thanks – but out in the passage she told me when I was next to visit her, some three or four days ahead.

I had not thought of her often before that version of a poetry reading, now I could think of almost nothing else. She was not my love – I loved another, a virginal girl of my own extended family and class. I was also in love with an imaginary unknown goddess, but Mrs Jones had charms associated with propinquity, experience, interest in me, and was compatible inasmuch as we had breathed in unison. Not in love tho' I thought myself, I suffered from the doubts of lovers that were new to me. What next – what did she mean, what did it – would we, could we – was I capable, would she allow? I counted the hours until my return to the house in a terrace with its front door on the pavement, and the parlour almost lacking the room to swing a cat, and the other sordid appurtenances on which my desires were fixed.

Anti-climax was the name of that visit. I assumed that her unspoken message was *Enough*, for she was as inattentive as her husband said I was, absent-minded, restless, hard to talk to, and refused to fill silences. I was shy, and did not blame her for transmitting her shyness to me – and I remembered my position in relation to hers, and failed to guess that she was also recollecting the dangerous aspects of our association. I was not in love with my head, but another part of my anatomy whispered otherwise – the consequence was disappointment for me.

I was dismissed early – she had no time for poetry. Out in the passage, in the shade by the front door, she said sorry for not having been good company, and I drowned her apologies with my own. She stopped and faced me with her hand on the doorknob, looked into my eyes fair and square, and caressing my cheek with her free hand she reached up and kissed my lips, saying *For a Poet*. Then she opened the door and almost pushed me from her house.

The sequence of events escapes my memory – what matter? – all that needs telling is that the aphrodisiac Time, together with scholastic duties and marital appointments, kept us waiting. We were in that area of love that goes by the title Foregone Conclusion – considered by many more satisfying than Cat and Mouse or Consummation – but I was not to know these comparative points of the play of love – and simply grew keener by the day. I was not exactly alone in such amorous regions – had become a regular visitor to the Jones' residence, first by appointment, then by permission to call at teatime on weekdays when the householder was always teaching – and an element of slightly tense humour had insinuated itself into my ever closer relations with its mistress who was not yet mine. She spoke my Christian name sometimes, and once claimed to be my godmother, with which appellation I strongly disagreed, being sick of motherhood, and again she would call me Robin, from Robin Hood, since her Christian name was the same as that of Maid Marian. She decided I was still growing taller, and teased me by making us stand back to back while she balanced a book on her head – she was responsible for more jokes than I, for I could not be so free with her as vice versa.

Once in these outwardly harmless days we were disturbed by the entry of Jones who had forgotten some book with which to bore a class of his to distraction – he showed astonishment, he exaggerated it, to find me *in situ*, while I could not stop myself blushing, and the lady showed a hard defiance I had not seen in her before. Jones said he was deeply honoured that Lord Byron should be so unassuming as to set foot in his home, and his Missis snapped that she was compensating for her Mister's attempt to downgrade Lord B. into a postman. Might Jones ask what the purpose of His Lordship's visit now was, since no delivery of corrective essays was – for a change – required? Lord B. had been repaying her minor acts of hospitality by letting her see his poetry. Oh so it was poetry, was it? – says Jones – adding that opti-

56

mism in the direction of Lord B. becoming a true poet was misplaced in his humble opinion. Well, says the Missis, he could keep his opinion to himself, for he knew nothing of poetry, and was a Philistine of the first order – and she would appreciate it if he would fetch his blessed book and begone. Against my expectations, this episode did not lead to more of Jones' snarls at me in the classroom – he kept quiet, and confined his reaction to my friendship with his wife to occasional baleful looks – he might have been complaisant for all I knew, even if there was not yet much cause to complain.

Should I begone too, should I desist from visiting, I felt obliged to inquire. – No, she emphatically told me – she would give me notice when it would be tactful to stay away – otherwise I was to continue as before – tho' she would rearrange future visits by word of mouth – an excess of notes in her writing might provoke gossip. Thus the conspiracy developed – a relief mutually, and how stimulating to share secrets with an adult female who had kissed me! Once she demanded to know if I boasted of seeing her to other boys – no, I promised, trying to convey my semi-conscious understanding that privacy heightens passion – and she provided corroboration by speaking of our own little world. In fact, my schoolfellows scarcely noticed my absences of an hour or two – we all had different fish to fry in our free time, sports and hobbies.

What was the turning point? Nothing is truer

than that intimacy between one person and another seldom if ever remains in the singular. Mrs Jones foreshadowed my destiny inasmuch as she made the overture and she was the one who kissed – and I betrayed my weakness and my manhood by pursuing the will-of-the-wisp that flickered ahead and inflamed me. One day she announced that Jones was departing to attend his ailing mother in Wales, would be gone for a fortnight, and I could look in on her as I pleased – without, of course, alerting her neighbours with their wagging tongues.

My visitations were definitely the postponement of pleasure as the fortnight progressed – we were sharpening our appetites for each other – or else it was like shadow boxing – or, in my innocence, like sailing over the horizon in search of a new land or nothingness. – Excitement possessed me, but I still had a schoolboy's appointments. To take part in football and other sport was necessity in consideration of the handicap of my foot. I always wished to prove my fitness, and in a game of football, the Harrow sort, I wrenched my back in a clumsy fall in muddy ground, and limped my injury along to where I knew it would receive sympathy and care.

Her alarm was almost excessive, but hypocritical. I was in pain, she truly said, must rest my back, lie flat, and she would apply embrocation – she would help me upstairs. Her help was already an embrace – we reached her bedroom – but the wet mud was still on my football clothing – she drew the curtains, told me to remove

58

my clothes and lie face downwards on the bed while she fetched hot water and the ointment to apply to the small of my back. I did not demur – she urged me not to be prim – she could at least dry my short trousers – and she would return in a moment. The bed scarcely had room for two – it suggested that Jones slept elsewhere – anyway I lay in the middle and as instructed in order to conceal my embarrassing loss of control over myself.

She washed what she could see of me with the hot water and began the anointing – but could not reach me as I was in the middle – while I was fairly stuck because of my injury – the consequences were first that she knelt alongside and soon that she apologised for straddling my thighs the better to apply the embrocating stuff to my spine. We were in close contact – and, for all my ignorance, I suspected that she had removed her undergarments and that it was her private flesh now touching mine. The movements of her hands slowed down and grew sensual – we stopped speaking – the darkness we were in hid barriers – and in silence her hands indicated to me that I was to turn over. – When I had done so, a movement of hers unravelled for me the last major riddle of the adult universe – and she subsided upon and almost submerged me in the flood of her tears.

Mrs Jones – Marian as I was about to call her – unriddled one riddle and immediately riddled another – what in the name of heaven and hell was she crying for?

Oh we had it out, no fear – for her the physical act was only completed by wordy emotion. The answer to the riddle of her behaviour *post coition* was the lesson men have to learn, that if women were comprehensible they would not be different, and if they were the same as their lovers they would be less loved. I asked the question posed succinctly by Hamlet, *What was the matter?* I made the mistake of youth by worrying that I had hurt her. No no, said she – she cried because she was happy, because she had been so unhappy for so long, because her marriage was a mockery, because she felt guilty, a wicked wife, a bad woman to have seduced me – even if it was my fault, not hers – because I was temptation and would be the downfall of womankind.

I wiped away her tears, and soon was guided by Marian and by nature towards the only unfailing cure for a sensitive female in distress. I cannot pretend that repetition was unselfish where I was concerned – addiction was already my discovery and the onset of my curse. – The realisation that I was not a cold fish from the North Sea, not the kind of Englishman who gets sex out of his system on his honeymoon and afterwards treats his wife like his housekeeper, was seeded in my mind and grew by confirmation in future years. Whilst my recently acquired mistress was explaining herself at some length, calm descended on me after the storm of the last weeks, and that rationality which is the enemy of romance. My knowledge of the lady had been specialised – for to start with she had been Jones' wife and then she became my titillator and the object of desire, whose intellect and character were not my business.

Her untruthfulness detracted from the esteem in which I had inclined to hold her – she lied to accuse me of having seduced her – I was so far the passive contributor and she the active one – besides, she was old enough to know the language of love. Latin peoples are well aware that the touch of skin on skin, let alone kisses on lips, is fraught with danger – girls are taught to keep their hands to themselves, while men believe that a womanly pat is a proposition.

Marian Jones was born a Smith – her surnames were commoner than she was – she was the daughter of teachers, yet had a nervous system more refined than those usually found on the dais of classrooms – but her brow was middle and her class middle-middle. She approved of my verse but also of doggerel in greeting cards from the seaside – she gave me a premonitory introduction to the disillusionment of authors who find that the admirers of their work also admire the work of their despicable competitors and rivals. She was sentimental – no bad thing in a woman in itself – but indiscriminately so – and allied in her to a streak of ruthlessness. The pictures on the walls of her house were of idealised cottages and rustic couples holding hands in the sunset, and again of the male gods of Ancient Greece unclothed and bloody battles replete with wounded soldiery. Her furnishings aimed at but fell below fashion, and revealed impecuniosity.

She had the nous to be able to trace her disgruntlement to source. Her husband's Christian names were Theodore Wilfrid – a nominal warning to wiser women surely. – She had been twenty-two – against her wishes and hopes she had followed in her parents' footsteps – she began to teach in school – and Theodore was older than she was, and she thought cleverer, and flattered her with his interest, and obtained her father's support. – She ascribed to him the virtues she imagined, and knew he was better than the nothing that was otherwise on offer – and she was impatient too – her body propelled her in his direction. The communing of a male virgin of forty and a healthy intact girl of twenty-two was as difficult in practice as in theory. Theodore Jones felt it beneath his dignity to struggle for success and risk failure – and his spouse's efforts to obtain satisfaction shocked him and were repelled with the energy that was errant in the other connection or disconnection.

Oh and ah, how hungry she had been! She confessed the details of her private life immodestly – I lacked the wit or the authority to restrain her. She had lived in a vacuum, a wife in name only, robbed even of parental affection, losing her chances of maternity with every day and night that passed, trying in vain to make the best of the impossibility of escape. – She was shamed to recall the misdemeanours of her loneliness, her wilder acts inspired by frustration, the eyes of strange men she had caught, a ten-minute exchange behind a tree in a London park in the dark. She had been ready for any-thing when she met me, she disclosed with fool-hardy tactlessness. But I was this and I was that – and how was she to resist, baby-snatching tho' she could be charged with? – I was the stuff of her dreams, for it was the common knowledge of women that boys of my age were more potent than their seniors – I was the prize or blessing somehow won or awarded to the poor in spirit.

One of her ideas of me was not wrong at that time of my life – but men are not meant to boast about it. I was insatiable – and satiety is seldom suffered by her sex – and I could well claim that for both of us a single objective com-mandeered our processes of thought. I returned to the charge again and again – at dawn, in day-light warily, and stole out of my house to be with her for long enough at night – this was in the fortnight of her Theodore's sojourn in Wales. We exhausted each other – it was more than sat-isfaction – and the phrase in the Holy Bible relative to the giving to those that hath and the taking away from those that hath not applies most accurately to carnal experience – women's beauty is increased by intercourse and their beauty reconquers men. My ideals fell to earth, pedestals cracked – my yearnings were for the anatomy of Marian Jones, positioned one way or another, without delay.

Alas, Theodores are like bad pennies and will turn up – and Marian moaned and mourned, interfering with my pleasure. – I could barely bring myself to console her, for I had no ambition to fill the lowly post of the prop of her marriage – and to borrow a phrase of hers that had acted as keystone of our affair, I was not averse to a *breather*. She had been educative, generous, an ever ready accomplice, the first to prove to me that not all women were like my mother, my most influential schoolmistress, if I may link her with Harrow and my initiation to Venusian rites – but no orgy can be endless, I had work to do, and my vocation recalled me to its service. What was not in her favour was that another of her phrases, which had been drowned by the noises of ecstasy, now beat discordantly on my eardrums – she insisted on asking if I loved her – *Did I love her a little?*

It had not weighed on my mind, the concept of love, if my mentality had ever been drawn into our physical communion. – Her question in all its unfriendly complexity disconcerted me – not to be mealy-mouthed, I was quite disgusted – loving Mrs Jones was never what I had been thinking about, and I did not distract myself by trying to divine her deeper thoughts on the subject of our labours. Love for me remained the unattainable ideal, a spiritual quest, utterly divorced and different from our earthy sessions. Throughout my conscience had been untroubled by the idea of infidelity to my dearest cousin, which is the gauge of my separation of the two activities.

If these pages should chance to fall into the white hands of women, which are noted for their tenderness and mercy, I quail to imagine their appreciation of my duality. – *Typical of his sex* would be their least belligerent comment – dishonest, dishonourable, cruel and beastly, they would shrilly judge. In my defence I can only put forward the claim that there is nothing so stupid as ignorance. I might have crossed and recrossed the Rubicon, but I was not near the consolidation of love with heart and soul and the rest of the *corpus*. – Mrs Jones began to weld me together, no doubt, but received no gratitude for upsetting the apple cart of my solitude and its dreamy requirements. Did I love her a little? *Would she repeat that?* Well, I was not absolutely sure – I was sorry to be impolite – she must give me time to answer – I supposed so – perhaps, a little. Naturally she was not content with my grudging lack of co-operation in this area, when I was being so ready to meet her halfway in another. She badgered me to show an enthusiasm of the verbal variety equal to the corporeal – the consequence of which was that I loved her less than I would have done if she had not introduced strife and force into our dealings.

Jones came home and afforded me some rest. Again I was not grateful, and, when he stared or glared at me in class, topsy-turvily I blamed him for not acknowledging that I had relieved him of matrimonial duty. After a few days, Marian Jones summoned me to compensate for the omissions of every sort of her husband – not a very romantic errand. I warned her that I would not be at her beck and call in future since trials and scholastic tests approached – at which she grew hysterical, and was brought to her senses by my warning her that passers-by would imagine murder was in train, and by the imminence of Jones clocking in for his evening meal. – I had another discouraging string to my bow, I told her that my comrades had started to show interest in my absenteeism from our games and play-times, that her good name had to be protected, and therefore it was essential that I should reduce the number of my visits to her home. – Her cries of despair were quickly replaced by her suspicions and harsh demand, *Had I been boasting of my Conquest?* I denied it hotly, the heat arising from my resentment of her distrust.

The next event, unforgettable rather than memorable, was a note addressed to me despite her cautiousness and mine BEGGING – underlined ten times – me to attend her with minimum delay. I sighed and obeyed, not pleased with her for causing me apprehension, tho' my imagination had not extended to the awfulness of the reason why I needed to be apprehensive. – She opened the door – a changed being hustled me indoors – white face, red eyes, a stooping broken form – nothing remained of that which I had at least worshipped with my body – the cause probably obvious to all except me –

she blurted out that she feared she was having our baby.

How I hated that news! The pronoun *our* was like a sword thrust – the *baby* was a succubus crushing me – it was all objectionable, but how to object? – I was ignorant even of the facts of a woman's life, and biology was a closed book.

A conversation predictably horrible ensued. What did she mean? She cursed me for pretending not to know. What would happen, what would she do? No, sir, no, what had I done to her and what were my intentions? I suggested in some roundabout way that I intended nothing, and it was not my pigeon. She called me a fool, a cruel fool for not realising that she would have to inform her Theodore who would probably throw her on to the streets: What then, sir – will you stand by me? I refused to cross that bridge prematurely, and got my face slapped for not immediately offering to ruin my life on her account. She chucked words at me as if they were brickbats – shame, outcast, poverty, starvation, suicide – and supplied a kind of punctuation by bouts of crying and imploring me not to desert her altogether, for she adored me and had given me her all, etcetera etcetera.

I cannot conceal that after the first shock subsided my sole aim was to get away from her as soon as the odd pairing of politeness and selfishness permitted. Help from me was out of the question – she could have saved her breath to cool her porridge, as my mother had often advised her only child. Marian was neither unmarried nor marriageable, and I was saved from having to consider matrimony by my age – anyway poets do not marry young, and never should marry till they cease to versify – they must remain free to break the bonds of senseless laws and absurd conventions. Moreover, since nature is not kind, I might as well record that my natural reaction to her despair was to find her unattractive to the point of repulsiveness and to wonder at my intimate conjunctions with that stringy elderly mop of hopeless blubbing. Eventually I disentangled myself from her arms and escaped, celebrating in the open air until darker clouds reassembled over my head.

I foresaw publicity – Jones on the warpath – my role in the affair revealed and ridiculed – my sacking, my rustication, and the gentle condolences I could expect from my next of kin. – I linked crime and punishment by means of my experience, and dreaded in particular the humiliation of a whipping from the Headmaster of Harrow School. The form of my response to *our* baby was to regret the making of it and to hope to see and hear no more of its mother.

But a day or two later I did hear again or, rather, read in yet another note she should not have dropped on me the phrase that for all its brevity has struck umpteen men as the most beautiful in our language, *All Right.*

Relief allowed me to accede to her request for another meeting – as she put it, I had to meet her again – and at the appointed time I retraced my steps to the terrace house, where I was whisked indoors even more briskly than usual. She looked better and had recovered her affection for me, but proceeded to treat me to a lesson in biology I would have preferred not to have to learn – I was not spared the belated blood.

Her apologies for sharing her worries were accompanied by her keenness to kiss and make better – her heat warmed me, and soon we agreed to continue our *discussion* up the stairs and in the bedroom. – But love was constrained by events, she dared not risk a repetition of pregnancy of the false sort, not to speak of the genuine article – she tried to muzzle me in a metaphorical manner – unsatisfactory compromises were resorted to and resisted – and nothing was the same. We did try to make the best of a bad job, she promised to be more accessible, I to have another shot, and we fixed a further date for meeting, according to custom.

I was agreeable because the end of my winter term was in sight, I was not due to return to Harrow, and therefore could indulge Marian again without danger, apart from that which might result from telling her we would have to say adieu for ever. – I owed her a spot of kindness, to repay hers – after all I had enjoyed her services at no cost.

While we lay together, preparatory to dressing, the worst or almost the worst, the possible worst which we had complacently ceased to fear, happened – the front door opened, male voices in conversation were audible, and Jones called for his wife. – He was early, he was with his superior master, Spolforth by name – she could recognise Spolforth's way of talking – Jones had brought Spolforth home for supper, as arranged, but two hours before they were expected – so I gathered from her gasping out the horror of her predicament and incidentally mine. We were trapped fair and square – no flight over the leads for me as for Casanova – too far to jump from her window – excuses alone might extricate us. We threw on clothes – she pinched her blanched cheeks to restore a rose or two – she clasped my hand despairingly – and we descended the stairs.

Jones and Spolforth were in the parlour. For a moment it seemed as if his Missis and my Mistress could cause me to vanish without discovery. But Jones emerged into the passage and we confronted one another – he too startled to speak, myself too afeard that I might say the wrong thing, and Marian gabbling that I had been helping her to look for embrocation for pain in my back – and then Spolforth, a large dark scowling man, joined us. Introductions followed in the style of a garden party – I shook the hand of Spolforth – and Jones inquired with a menacing inflection, *May I show Your Lordship out of my house?* I thanked him and departed. But it was not the end of the story for out in the street I heard the cry of the cuckold, which was more like bellowing, and knew that an epilogue was bound to follow.

A day or two later, in the morning, a note arrived for me in the hand I recognised from corrections of my school exercises. – It ran, *My Lord, Pray come to my house at six sharp, T.W. Jones.* Marian awaited me in the parlour – the eternal triangle was fully represented – she sat on the sofa with head bowed and hair disarrayed – the owner of his castle took his stand in front of the unlit fire, and I remained on my feet, waiting for my sentence.

From memory, our exchanges were as follows. *Jones* – You have done irreparable damage to my wife and to me, sir. Have you anything to say for yourself?

B. – Your wife is not to blame.

Jones – I regret to say that in my opinion you over-estimate your powers of attraction. You may be a Lord, but I have always thought you less noble than you presume you are. I must ask you not to strike poses before me.

B. – And I must ask you not to insult me.

Jones – Insult you! I would fight you and gladly kill you if I were willing to run the risk of leaving a penniless widow and yielding up my life to a worthless boy. You are irresponsible and callous, my Lord. You were caught in a compromising situation with my wife by myself and Mister Spolforth, and you seem to choose to overlook the consequences personal and professional.

B. – We were looking for embrocation ——

Jones – You lie, sir! Mrs Jones lied to me, and not for the first time. You and she plotted together to ruin me. I have already tendered my resignation to the Headmaster, who requested me to spare him the embarrassment of giving me the sack.

B. – I cannot help it if Mr Spolforth told tales.

Jones – My neighbour had already reported the goings-on in my house. You were as careless as you are callous, sir. I believe you were determined to be revenged for my finding fault with you in class.

B. – Mr Jones, you mistake me – I bore you no malice – you could not hurt me – you are misinterpreting events.

Jones – For once you are right. No, I could not hurt a peer with wealth and a fine estate. But I am not so lucky as you are, my Lord – I have or I had little except my tutorial post – can you not grasp the meaning of the word ruination? Are you blind to the misery of my wife, and can you not imagine the blight you have cast upon my professional standing and future? Open your eyes, my Lord, and look upon the tragedy you and my wife have engineered between you!

B. – I am not rich, Mr Jones, –

Jones – That is the last straw, sir – I will not accept payment for what you have been doing to my wife – I am not so low as you suggest – out of my house, if you please! You may bid your colleague in adultery goodbye, and do not forget that if you ever speak to her again or she to you I shall evict her from my lodging and my life, and let her seek her fortune where she belongs, thanks to you – on the streets.

That was all, Jones had spoken – he now brushed past me to open his front door, leaving the door of the parlour open.

Marian at last raised her head and, showing me her blotched face, said she must look at me once more – to which I mumbled a reply intended to be sympathetic.

My Lord, says Jones by the front door, *I am impatient to see the backside of you.*

On the way out I might have said I was sorry, but he moved as if to kick me and I hurried off with my tail between my legs, as the saying goes.

Here endeth the first Lesson descriptive of my apotheosis into demon lover who writes poetry in his spare time – an inglorious destiny, forsooth. But since I have been asked a thousand times how and why I became a poet, and how I lost my soul – the latter question by ladies who would assist me to find it – I will oblige again, for my obliging nature is the real villain that emerges from my biography. Tho' I am not one of your whining rhymers who devastate the *sensitive* readers of today, and despite my conviction that we are all about to analyse ourselves out of existence, I will go against my principles and my temper and pick myself to pieces in the next pages.

There were a few more weeks of Harrow ahead, and beyond that Cambridge beckoned. My first response to the last climax of the formation of my addiction to love in the raw was thankfulness to be rid of the Joneses. I had been feeling I was due for partition between the left and right claws of a crab – and was free, I thought, without subjecting freedom to closer examination, and had nothing more to fear. The tattle was that Jones had resigned on the grounds of the ill health of his wife, and the happy fact for me was that they had removed from their house, a property owned by Harrow School and tied to the work of its masters.

Without Mrs Jones to have to make love to or Mr Jones to consider, a celebratory mood took hold of me, relative not to liberty but to the achievements of my captivity. – My constitution is of the type, recognised by artists if not by the general, that can enthuse in anticipation of the future and enjoy recollections appertaining to the past, but is not made to drain the present to the dregs, is incapable of surrendering to its ups and downs, and without exaggeration and more than anything else *endures* it. I had known the enthusiasm of the beginner in female arms that had neither chance nor inclination to clasp the wormlike physique of Theodore Wilfrid, and made the acquaintance of passion – that is, lust – and turned to manfully when taught the intricacies of the task. But mere spontaneity was revealed as misleading by the force of my fervour in retrospect. – My solitude was shot through with beams of unqualified pleasure and accompanied by choruses of self-congratulation. The uncertainty dinned into my childhood by the sweet whisperings of my mother was sloughed like an old skin, and I looked outwards for a change with confidence – I had proved that women could be subdued and that I was armed with weapons for their subjugation.

– I make no apology for the callousness of the above. If my readers are unaware that youth, the male version in particular, is exclusively selfish, and that even noble lords are apt to fail the test of altruism and self-denial, I would beg them to return to their studies of the flat earth and the green cheese that shines at night.

– But for those who can bear to contemplate naked villainy, a redeeming feature or a piece of *poetic* justice is in view. The wonder of my apprenticeship to the reality of love, the discovery of what it could cost me, and the scorching humiliation of the final lesson taught me by Jones, all incurred expense of effort. – I had prodigally squandered my substance – a great reaction set in, exaltation was replaced by abasement, and powerful weakness overwhelmed me. A desolation never before known informed my thoughts – it possessed my being utterly. I pleaded sickness and lay in bed for days, sleepless and beyond comfort. At length it yielded to an omnipresent melancholy, yet another of the novel experiences of this unique time of my life.

In short, and as my friends would corroborate, thus was established the pattern of my adult existence to date – violent effort and exuberance succeeded by despair mutating slowly into melancholia, and repetitions of the cycle.

To confess that I was alarmed by the shifting sands I apparently stood on is an understatement, and matters were not mended by recollecting my infidelity to dearest Mary and by wishing I had not been caught by an inferior with my hand in his matrimonial till. It was too late, I had passed the point of no return – such was the refrain of my elegiac reflections – and what was to be done, what was I good for, except the waste-pit?

I turned to poesy – recalled my essays in that line – and my boyish ambition to be a poet. – I turned and realised I was *returning* to the solace of my miserable cohabitation with my mother – I gained my first conscious intuition that on the blank page I could create and re-create my true and only home. Not joy ensued from the discovery – I was not in the joyful key – but the feeling that I had reached *terra firma* and could re-engage in activity since I was in no danger of losing my balance. I wrote with a fortunate fluency for myself – for dear life – and through the troughs and torments in store for me I was again and again drawn back to my desk, where I maintained my prolific style.

Subject matter has been a by-product of the melancholic mood that has depressed and inspired me. Neither the cheerfulness of the face I show the world, nor the morbidity of some of my work, are lies – they are the likeness of the two-headed Janus that I am. At Harrow, before I left it for Newstead and Cambridge, I recovered laughter to share with my friends and a taste for games and even for scholarship, but I scribbled in private sombrely – I stole away to be alone with my sadder vision of humanity. A poem dating back to those days has won some praise, tho' more because I was young to write it than because it is passably good – the so-called *Lines written beneath an elm in the Churchyard of Harrow*. The incomplete excerpt I copy here sums up the self that emerged from the transformations and troubles, the extremities of sensation, I have described –

> When fate shall chill, at length this fever'd
> breast,
> And calm its cares and passions into rest.

– Little did I imagine that now, years later, in my maturity, I would be forced to look over my shoulder at the half-witted lechery of my youth, and to suffer a delayed pang of sympathy with the victims of high and low jinks.

PART TWO

I have scribbled one of the two histories in my head. Taken together, they aim to be a wry comparison of youth with age of general interest and application. But I would not have written the first if I had not been reminded of it by the *dénouement* of the second. That I am determined and yet unwilling to tell all, not being a lover of pain, is attested to by my need of procrastination.

The next paragraphs refer to a tragedy of sorts, but in truth are beside the revelatory point I would make.

Recently, my Harrovian acquaintance, Wilson by name, known as Wilson Minor in our schooldays, took a peep at Venice in the course of his tour of the Continent and felt obliged to roust me out at an inconvenient time. – Not content with disrupting my routine and disturbing my work, Wilson overstayed his welcome after five minutes in which he managed to upset me by retailing news of the Joneses. He did not know the half of it – but innocently related that after Jones retired from schoolmastering at Harrow he was employed by Wilson's parents to tutor a younger Wilson brother, Wilson Minimus, of singular ineptitude – consequently the Wilson family kept up with the Joneses for several years – until Jones died soon after the premature

death of his wife. When was that, I asked –
oh, says Wilson, five or six years after we left
Harrow. – And did Wilson know Mrs Jones? –
indeed, a pretty woman, says he, who went
downhill steadily and passed away before she
had hit forty. – I then thanked the little beast
for bringing me bad news and begged him to
leave.

Marian dead – not that it was exactly her
death that distressed me – we would all die of
mourning if we were to suffer on account of the
death of everyone we ever played with – the dis-
tressing part was that after only not much more
than a decade and a half she was almost a blank
in my memory.

What did we talk about? Why, the weather –
we were English. Did we discuss poetry? No, for
I cut short her pretentious chatter on the subject. Did we laugh together? Yes, but only *en
route* to bed. What did she look like? I remember her labia better than her lips, and another
pair of protuberances better than the colour of
her eyes. But she was a woman new to me in
the most important of ways, a kind woman, and
may she rest in peace.

At Harrow, after she and I were torn asunder
by Theodore Wilfrid and I had recovered my
health and poise, I was glad to get on with my
work, and the same applies to her brief resur-
rection through the medium of Wilson Minor.
Writing was, has been and is my truest love, tho'
we grow sometimes a little sick of each other.

Now, pen in hand as usual, I can unravel the

mystery of my romantic life once again, before it ruffles more feminine feathers and causes more heartburn. I versified when I was hit by Cupid's dart, but I would not succumb to wounds, would work the harder at my verses, and could not write and make love simultaneously – there in a nutshell has been the fault found in me by the ladies. I won love in order to have reason to reject it – what an unwise confession, enough to stand the ladies in a long queue, each anxious to show that she is able to put a collar on me and bring me to heel. But I never will be led, I also have a poetic soul to lose, I survived my mother and emancipated myself from her domination – and the same story has been repeated many times already, and will be as long as I have breath in my body and the wherewithal to scribble.

Love was no trouble in the years when I sought the friendship of the traitor, fame. The city of Cambridge teemed with girls willing to keep undergraduates happy at low cost without interrupting scholarship unduly – and at Newstead, when I recovered it from Lord Grey, village maidens lent extra amusement to the visits of my intimates. I paid for private publication of my poetry, and stood no nonsense from publishers, booksellers, reviewers and suchlike, middlemen who vandalise art if they are given the chance. But ambition drove me first to excel and then to have my excellence applauded – to compete was my second nature, and I would not be content unless I was at last to be top of the class. I made a stir when I tackled the Scotch detractors of my wares, the jackals who pick the bones of poets in the columns of the Edinburgh Review, and I sealed my fate with *Childe Harold*.

I had been carving a niche for myself in the London of sociabilities suited to my name and interests. Overnight I was transmogrified into the spare man most wanted by the social spirits who float above the common ground – I was rich despite my debts, popular beyond my worth, admired even for my shortcomings, and invited to entertain the high and the mighty. The social classes in England could be the subject of a monograph of a few thousand pages – they make complexity look like child's play – they are a cat's cradle of contradictions – a secret withheld from the populace, the despair of foreigners, defying description even to initiates. There are a labouring class, a middle and an upper, or so neatness wishes; but, setting aside the two that would deny they are lower, within the upper class are innumerable gradations. – Aristocrats can be social outsiders, boorish, bankrupt – their titles can die out, they can become no different from everyman – shunned because of their presumption, and sliding down the social ladder.

The intricacies of the upper class do not stop there – some members bear names without handles, they belong to an untitled aristocracy raised by the possession of old lands and old money, and are blessed simply because they are included. Other gentlemen with neither land nor money, nor aristocratic connections, have been known to penetrate the select circle – they are the clowns, who crack the jokes or are the butt of jokes, the favourites, the *good causes*; – and ladies, too, can squeeze in on a couple of alternative accounts, because they please His Lordship or because they are unlikely to please him. Who decides, who rules this roost swaying about at the top of the social tree? – Occasionally a male, a grandee, whose least word is law – not any royal personage but one of those dukes who look down on royalty and are firmly convinced they have prior rights to the throne. – More often, as a rule, a clique of clever ladies with too much energy, resources, time on their hands, ability going to waste, gregarious inclinations, ruthlessness and disciplinary traits. They issue the invitations, they grant favours and withdraw their favour, they set the fashions and are courted by those without the pale – neither young nor old, governing socially and usually politically too through their husbands, they are the Queen Bees of a small hive of four or five hundred workers and drones – and they wield extraordinary influence over the wider world.

In Paris during the Revolution the ladies who ruled were barely out of their teens, they were lucky enough to have young husbands willing to cut off the heads of aristos and a harmless Queen, and they lived on the fat of the land while everyone else starved – but they did put a stop to the mindless murders, and then Bonaparte came along to reinstate the old social order with a touch of Corsican bad taste. Across the English Channel, in our heaven on earth, society was in the more wrinkled hands of matriarchs, ladies who would admit to being a year or two older than their French counterparts, and had enough sensibility and humour and sensuality and giddiness to get any green poet into trouble. – I write, of course, of the social whirl into which I was plunged on the day after the publication of *Childe Harold*, Cantos I and II.

Was it for literature that I was invited into the marble halls and sumptuous salons of the great hostesses? Was it for art that I was press-ganged to eat ices nightly to the squawks of violins? Strange indeed that such busy females with their exacting husbands, spoilt children, palaces and armies of servers to look after, and parties and other people's lives to arrange, and bodies to wash, and fittings for clothes to hang on them to be fitted in, and above all hair to be seen to daily – strange that they should still have time to read the published poetry of a beginner while the ink was hardly dry and to bother to bid the poet to an *urgent* supper in his honour!

There is no denying that I differed in some respects from the ordinary run of poets, who have a tendency to be common, or on the dry academic side, or dwarf-like, or ugly, and to be violently radical until they either find a rich protector or starve to death in their garrets. British phlegm does not allow a man to boast that he is or was pretty, but it may sound better to suggest that the ladies in question had heard of my *beaux yeux*. Rumours could have spread from the inky regions that I was capable of *flattering* a woman in between dashing off a Canto or two – and there was later evidence that the hope and expectation of *amours* of the personal, vicarious, amusingly scandalous or deliciously horrible sort had stirred superannuated senses to seize a pen and summon me to partake in the orgiastic revels of the higher ladies of the town.

I was not so sardonic in those days. My adorable mother was dead, but her parting shot to me could have been to curse me with an eagerness to suffer and, missing the yoke of herself, to shoulder readily the burden of acquaintanceship with a dangerous set, composed of elders and betters in the upper echelons, nearer my own age down below. My mother's snobbery, which refused to see the cloven hoof of Lord Grey de Ruthyn, and her Scotch relentlessness, combined to make me happy to accept invitations from a Duchess by one delivery, from a Countess by another, from a pitiful Lady by the next, and from peers of all descriptions who wrote on behalf of their peeresses. My parents between them had bequeathed to me two further traits that had some appeal – an extravagantly virile energy, tireless in its flowering tho' apt to wilt before long, witness the early deaths of both my Pater and Mater, and secondly a club foot and a limp, which deformity, in accordance with the well-known perverseness of the feminine nature, implanted romantic, curious and libidinous ideas in the minds of my new patrons.

To confess that I was the toast of everywhere would be almost an understatement. Success, added to the contents of the previous paragraph, guaranteed that more than matriarchal interest would be taken in me *tout de suite.* The competitors were after my blood, those fair mild soft-skinned and soft-hearted creatures who will pursue and sink their teeth into any man so that no sister of theirs will get him. They would have eaten me alive if they could – they almost did – but Lady Caroline Lamb pranced into view with teeth bared and her claws out – and tho' she was half their size and a quarter of their weight she shooed them off and nibbled me nearly to death.

The story is stale buns, which I will not serve up again in its entirety. – My object is herein to record a few extenuating factors not generally known. Caro Lamb was a *charmer* beyond compare in the opinion of the sophisticates who bred her, made far too much of her, called her crimes an effusion of spirits, and admired her uncritically. It was as if they conspired together to re-edit her to suit themselves, and to create a heroine out of a few shreds of candy floss. When I first set eyes on her, far from being knocked over by her appearance and personality, I thought her peculiar, an urchin with an unmelodious drawl, a *poseuse* if ever there was one with the short hair of a child infested by lice, attitudinising and acting as if pleased with herself for overwhelming but incomprehensible reasons.

We were introduced. Her mother Lady Bessborough or her mother-in-law Lady Melbourne, mother of Caro's husband William Lamb, brought her up to me – at her request, as I learnt later on. She was flighty, hoity-toity, as certain silly women are in hopes of provoking a man to rape them without more ado. She was short of stature, slight as a skeleton, and her hand, that powerful claw of hers, was like the foot of a sparrow to the touch – yet her blue eye was bright, there was an elfin brightness about her, and a promised fleetness of foot, useful when she crept out from beneath her mushroom at night and danced in the moonshine. Other women were waiting to pay me their homage, and she, on appreciating that I had to fulfil the duties of my popularity, flounced off with a toss of her tiny head.

I thought no more of that wife of another man – if I had I would have called to mind the cautionary tale of Marian Jones. I was unaroused to an inclusive degree, so scented not the merest whiff of peril. But she wrote to me, and how good she was on paper! How persuasive she could be when she was out to get her own way! No other woman, none of my female *suitors*, had written as she did, so well in the first place, and in the second with such emotional abandonment. She had to be with me, she insisted on another meeting, she demanded a *tête à tête*

– her meaning was made clear, the compliment was too strong for me – a top-notch lady abasing herself to my will, offering me herself on a plate, as indeed she actually did on a future occasion – it was too much for my obliging temperament.

Our assignation, while confirming my first impression, as is usually the case, introduced a new element into the equation of ourselves – her irresistibility. She was fey, affected, self-centred, unsatisfactory even in the course of our lovemaking, and in her nakedness she was as clothed, but the other side of her was her intense concentration on securing me, and her delighting me with her funniness, fancifulness, uniqueness, and ability to extract pledges galore as she dazzled with the display of her kingfisher colours. Fun is indescribable, tales of antics in the bedroom are unprintable, detailed accounts of copulation embarrass everybody above the age of consent, and the mere idea of making a joke of the procreation of children would shock Nordic puritans from top to bottom. – Therefore poor little Caro is a sorry loss to art, for she could be exquisite in her riggishness, and she stands no chance of being immortalised in any medium.

She was not, never had been, and had no cause to expect to be poor in any other respect. She had a head rich in invention, and was never short of the power to be active. Her conscience was undeveloped, as a result she was unworried by her lack of conscientiousness. She nicknamed her husband Silly Willy for my amusement. She was driven to play tricks on him with my assistance, seeking the limelight in my company so that William would see or hear of our exploits – or, if her husband and her lover happened to be in the same room somewhere, she would introduce the two of us with mock formality, now taking his arm, now mine. She was set on compensating for her smallness by scandalising the great world, and in the privacy of our love nests she cast such a crazy spell on me that I half-agreed with her that we should run away together and live as unhappily as the married couples ever after.

But she was bad at love, except love of herself. She was too thin to rise to the occasion in the act of loving, she lost herself nowhere along the primrose path, she studied to take rather than to give, and the sacrificial aspect of that activity did not impinge upon her consciousness – the only sacrifices she was associated with, tho' not acknowledged, were those made to her and for her by others. The enchantress who told delightful bedtime stories soon revealed that she was the wickedest imp alive.

One of many episodes convinced me we must separate as hurriedly as we had united. I had formed a bad professional habit of writing late at night or in the early morning – I was born a short sleeper, and my sociable instincts filled my days exclusively. Fame incurs a range of penalties, not the least of which for me was a publisher nagging me for more means to make money – Murray wished to know where were the other *Childe Harold* Cantos, and when could he expect them. I myself realised the transience of success, and that more must be done to feed the flames before which I had been warming my hands complacently. Caro respected my need to work to begin with, she boasted at routs and suppers that she was taking me away before midnight so that I could compose more death-less verse, implicitly verse in her honour. But I received the impression that she never slept at all, for she would disturb me at my solitary labours, pleading restlessness, pleading for proof of my love, and in short making a nuisance of herself.

The particular episode I have in mind had another twist. She arrived at twelve or in the smallest hours, obtained what she claimed she had wanted, and reminded me of the Wolborough ball, a lavish affair still in train at a mansion hard by. I showed no interest. She expressed a wish to return to the ball – we had looked in on the show earlier. At this hour? – Never, I replied. But she wished, she wanted it, she would not be rudely brushed aside. My work, said I, still patient. Could I, would I, not give up an hour or two of working – a little time out of a long life – for her sake, for her pleasure? My negative was firmer. She started to cry, to scream, she sank on a sofa in a false swoon, came to and drummed her feet on the floor, and then it was argument. – I did not love her, I was a seducer, a snob and social climber, had ink in my veins instead of blood, was heartless and cruel, deserved whipping, and she would expose me to everyone who counted and ruin me with relish. I rebutted her charges – and at length slapped her face – she was amazed, dumbfounded – silenced, tho' only for a minute – on a wave of her own tears she swept towards the window, pulled open the lower sash, and was climbing out intent on a painful suicide, since she would have landed on the spikes of my railings at street level.

I surrendered. As she was instantly cheerful, my surrender seemed worthwhile. We trotted to the Wolborough homestead and were soon engulfed in a sort of vortex of acquaintance. To this gang, My Lady now chose to announce in her carrying corncrake accents that I was not only the best poet and the most beautiful man in London, but also had a heart of unparalleled generosity, for I had desisted from writing at her behest, had given proof of affection at untold costs to genius and to pocket, and set a fine example of how women should be treated by their admirers. I was shamed, disgusted by praise of me that was actually self-praise, walked away, walked home alone and put the chain on my front door.

It was intolerable – other episodes emphasised the point that she was wrecking my existence and that she could no longer be tolerated. I applied for advice to my dear friend, Lady Melbourne – I was aware that she shared, and had reason to share, my considered opinion of the little person who had also dragged down her son. Marry, said she – a wife would protect me from Caro and the status of husband would entitle me to forgiveness for sowing wild oats. Who was I to marry, supposing I could bear to have a wife hanging round my neck and children's noses to wipe? She produced a candidate, Annabella Milbanke, a girl of infinite respectability, and undertook to find out how the land lay in that quarter. Ah well, I sighed, preparing to hand myself over with *unparalleled generosity* to another female – and permanently.

The answer that came back was negative. The lady declined, believe it or not. She might be respectable, well-bred and the rest of it, but she was a nobody and numskull – did she not know who and what was on offer?

The upshot of these events, *Childe Harold*, Caro Lamb and the disdainful one, was that I reacted from the excitement and effort by subsiding again into melancholy and misanthropy. My door was locked to all except my half-sister Augusta, wife of Colonel Leigh – her heart was like my own – we understood each other even too well, as things turned out in future. Augusta illuminated my dreary days, and persuaded me that my mistakes were not wholly foolish, and that I was honour bound to continue to write verses. Oddly, melancholy was not a destroyer of my work, on the contrary, and, as had already been established, lent it the essence, the flavour, that found favour with the public. I cannot remember the time scale of these developments, but, while I was still melancholic, I became the victim of one of the strangest plots ever plotted in the altitudinous reaches of society.

A number of ladies, a concentration of Countesses, banded together to beg me to resume relations with Lady Caroline Lamb. They were Christians, they knelt in church on Sundays, they were positioned to know better, they instructed the ignorant by example or were meant to, they should have been moralists, yet here they were, badgering me to recommit adultery. They did not say to me, sin or be damned – oh no, it was in the name of mercy, kindness, compassion that they wished me to be, they almost wished to see me, between the stringy shanks of another man's wife. Wonders never cease in society, and what could be more wonderful than the finest of the fair sex, who could not bear a single drop of grape juice to sully one of their fingers, hallooing me to have another shot at killing my fox, as if they had been licentious yokels having fun on a hunting day.

But who am I to mock and sneer? I was past caring what became of me and like some *blasé* customer in a whorehouse I eventually gave permission to the ladies in question to send in to me the person who concerned them.

Reheated meat always gave me indigestion. No doubt the same would have applied to Caro if she had ever eaten meat. We were at each other's

95

throats as soon as we had finished with our other parts. Her triumphs turned into tirades because I had dared to try to marry another woman, and my melancholia was deepened by her raging and ranting at me, and did not dispose me to have patience.

Typically, our talk that should have been grateful and tender as we lay in each other's arms after our exertions took the following course –

C. – Would you prefer to have done that to Annabella?

B. – Stop, I beg you, before we come to blows again – I have told you that I was misguided and then mistaken – I will say sorry once more if you insist – but I am not well, nor in the mood for fisticuffs.

C. – You seemed well enough ten minutes ago. Why do you complain of not being well? – I loathe ill health in others, and second to that I loathe pretence. You say you're not well to save yourself saying you love me.

B. – Fiddlesticks! You are mad – don't push me too far, I warn you.

C. – Strike me if it suits your coarse nature, a hot hit would be better than a cold kiss. – But you are right, I am mad to love you as I do, to lose my good name on your account, and to disgrace my family. – I am mad to have let you drive me into madness – tho' I am not so mad as not to know you still want me and that you never will get away from me – for one day I mean to kill myself at your feet and haunt you for ever!

B. – My lady, forgive my yawn. – Love upsets my stomach, Caro, do you hear me say so? Besides, you have no more love in you than a pig has poetry – laugh not, it's true in one sense, yet in another, I grant, you love me as property, because you love to think you are my proprietor. There! I must get up and you must leave me.

C. – What if I won't?

B. – Go, Caro, before I call the servants to carry you out.

C. – Please, I will make it worth your while to linger.

B. – No, Caro, I am sick of all the motions of loving. – And we are acting an error – steps in love can never be retraced – we are simply transforming our sweets into bitterness – we should agree to branch along our separate ways and remember the good times.

C. – I cannot bear that you will marry that stupid pudding, Milbanke.

B. – For God's sake, I am tired to telling you that you're wrong – the lady declined my most tentative offer – and you should know by now that I do not take kindly to an insult.

C. – Insult? What insult? You who claim to have a surfeit of insight into the workings of womankind are surely aware that no equals yes for us? Listen, listen, no I do not love you, no, I will no longer sanction things you have done to me, no, you shall not, you are not to put your hand there, unhand me, sir! Why, I have never been in a brothel, but the common talk is that a prostitute can bring a man to boiling point by means of denials, if all else fails. Annabella Milbanke must know men uncommonly well to try to catch a husband by turning him down.

B. – You are rattling, my dear. I have no time to listen to you.

C. – Don't leave me!

B. – Let go, Caro – I must work – we have finished, we are finished – adieu!

C. – If you pull that bell, it will toll for me, now *I* warn *you.*

B. – That is your business, I have to see to mine. For the last time, adieu!

C. – Oh you cruel, you wicked man –

So we went on until we lacked the inclination and the will to fight the old battles. We met, but not regularly, and love satisfied the less the more inventive and vicious it became – and my melancholy lifted to the extent of my half-reaching a decision that change was essential, if escape would not be allowed by the immoralisers in the seats of social power.

Caro was not always wrong – word reached me that Annabella regretted her rejection of my interest – and the pros seemed to outweigh the cons of matrimony to the *pudding.* – I would insist on my freedom to do as I pleased, drive the hardest bargain, and if she would sign on such a line I would let her be Lady Byron – no signature, nothing doing. But when we were better acquainted, tho' long before the wedding bells, it dawned on me that a moment after she opened her mouth to speak I was bored, whereas in a year of Caro's chatter, gossip, irrationality and possessiveness I never in fact suffered boredom – every other emotion, disagreement, impatience, rage and vain yearnings to flee, but boredom never. Consequently, during our *dealings* of the pre-marital variety, because I dreaded the soporific sound of her voice more than I had had my teeth put on edge by Caro's discordant drawling, and because I was already worn out by telling her what she did not begin to understand, I was the one who signed my name without bargaining or bothering to read the contents of any document – I was eager for nothing so much as to get it all over as quickly as possible.

Who now was mad? Caro and I in our wilder days had both had accusations of madness thrown in our faces – thrown not always by sanity. It had been the pot calling the kettle black, my repeated charges and my conviction that Caro was insane, since retrospect suggests that I married insanely. Well, talk of getting it over! That occurred in full, completely, at least in spirit, within hours of the ceremony – our first night was damn near our last – for I was so fired up by the absurdity of what I had been at, by the suicidal ill-judgment and carelessness of my conduct, that I rebelled and revolted against my wife's conventionality which was inflexibly resistant to passion, her chilliness which clothed itself in a mantle of modesty, and spoke to her in ways that made her hair stand on end and asserted my rights in the most far-fetched and frightening manner imaginable. – I made her share my impulses to cry, I justified with a vengeance Caro's conclusion that I was cruel, and laughed the new Lady B. out of the nuptial couch and into her closet, where she stayed till morning behind a locked door.

We were *together* for just over a year, that is to say we were mostly apart – and when we were united I would invite Augusta to join us and dilute the difficulty. Annabella understood nowt, and resented everything, Augusta's company and my close relations with my sister in particular. – Her pregnancy put a stopper on conjunction, and when Ada was born she fled to hide behind her mother's skirt and her father wrote to me about our legal separation.

I was relieved, but not for long. It was pleasant to have no wife, and my plans revolved round liberty and the unopposed opportunity to write – how green I still was in respect of the unwritten laws of the land into which fame had catapulted me! Admittedly I had tweaked the nose of society, still I would appeal against the severity of the punishment for my *crime*. Adulterers abound amongst the leisured class – indeed there is not much else for the members of that class to do – and it might be said that the minority consists of those who have never been adulterous – but I was singled out for the gravest disapproval on account of my treatment of Caro Lamb. – I had come between wife and husband – by my wiles had sorely wounded the happy little Lambs, according to the gossip, which was shouted from the rooftops by one of the two innocent creatures, while, from another rooftop, I was accused of addling the lady's brains by not attending to her nether organs.

I had done wrong, society said – meaning I was not to be allowed to protest that I could not do right in its biased judgment. Lenience was absolutely barred, no one would consider the fact that I relieved William Lamb of an intolerable burden, and redirected his wife's fire on to myself – and the fact that I had withdrawn in all senses from Caro was held very much against me. I was condemned for attracting her affection, for rejecting her affection, for cancelling that rejection, for renewing our liaison and for discontinuing it – I was like the woman accused of witchcraft and subject to the test of the village pond – if she did not drown she must be hanged and buried with a stake through her heart, if she was not a witch she died of drowning.

Consistency and loyalty are out of reach of the majority of our race – a truism truer than ever in a world ruled by frivolity and snobs. I do believe that literary leanings devalue a man in the eyes of the higher social animals – a bookworm is not so trustworthy as a landed gent or a good sport – and to dabble in art might pass for a social grace whereas success in such a field is next door to *trade*. My printed outpourings were a saucy adjunct to my amorous reputation, part of my equipment for ravishing the ladies, yet neither my poetry nor my performance really qualified me for admission into the best company. Who was I in comparison with Lady Caroline Lamb, whose family tree spread to the extent of a forest? – I was an upstart, a peer by mistake, son of a lunatic, and actually possessor of the equivalent of a cloven hoof.

The Countesses abandoned me to the extent of not owning up to their interference in my affair with Caro. In a genteel fashion, they threw me to the wolves who had been waiting for me to tumble into one of the many traps set for excessive success. They sided with the older firm, which had made its money long ago and closed its doors against an interloper. Perhaps I dramatise my situation at this stage of my fall from grace, yet thus it was that Annabella's evidence was so joyfully received.

Therein was confirmation of the opinions of the judicial mob – the shaky foundation of the charges levelled against me by my partner in the sin of adultery were vastly reinforced by the complaints of my wife. There, from the horse's mouth in common parlance, was proof that I was profligate and perverse, debauched and a debaucher of purity and chastity, not to mention my contrary treatment of virginity. Predictably enough, Annabella had seen none of my jokes during our treacle-moon – she always deserved nought for humour. My irony was lost on her – when I told her I loved her as much as I loved slugs and toads she took the compliment to heart, where it stayed until she could inform the universe that I loved slugs and toads more than the woman to whom I had made my vows before God a few hours previously. Those actions of mine on the first night of our intercourse which she termed *Unspeakable* were naturally spoken of and exaggerated in every drawing-room and tavern of the town. That I had got her with child, in view of my tastes, was considered quite a miracle by the technicians of love.

Not content with blackguarding me as husband, Her Ladyship arraigns me as brother, too. I had foisted my sister on to our early married days – I had shown a preference for chatting to my sister instead of getting to know my wife and giving her a chance to know me. – Whose fault was that, I wonder. – I had left the loveless marital bed to go and play games and to laugh with Augusta in her bedroom – whether or not our play was innocent was a moot point, according to the Milbanke clan and to my ill-wishers. In other words, to top up the long list of all that was wrong with me, I was incestuous.

That my relief was short-lived is scarcely surprising – I began to cower under the onslaught from a bitch and a dullard – more seriously, I saw clouds of another shape and colour advancing on the sun. Placed in a bad light by the slander of the ladylike, I could be or become an embarrassment to my few friends in the hierarchy – and at the same time my wickedness would be a candle to moths of the less desirable type of female, the sensationalists, the reformers.

The besmirching of my personality was again

a threat – my profession was threatened – my verse would be taken less seriously if it could be said, especially by critics, to be written by a gigolo. – My peerage, which had conferred the charm of unlikelihood on my creative powers, would be a liability if presented as my excuse for behaving badly and the privilege that had raised me above my rivals in the literary field.

All in all, when all has been said about my loves, my melancholia, and the mess of my affairs, I was sick of the totality of my life and even my good fortune. – I had exhausted the energy to enjoy myself, and was not over-anxious to correct the incorrigible or break my head against a wall. I hated England still more than it hated or for that matter loved me, and believed it would strangle my singing voice if I remained on its cold and clammy shores. The south summoned me, novelty and warmth held out a hand, and I seized it and went into exile without hesitation or tears.

The above may be stale buns, and I regret my weakness for yielding to the lure of self-justification. Yet why should I not have my say when everyone else in the world has had theirs? The better reason for running through events that are already public property to a degree, and probably should be left to the liars and biographers, is that I shrink from another chapter not revealed before and a secret that perhaps should be kept. But my *Diary* is bound to be a posthumous publication, if it ever sees the light of day – published long after my death by firm injunction and contract – and then interested parties will have joined me in heaven or hell. Why do what you yourself suggest ought not to be done, I am asked. Oh but the answer is surely clear, my record is my answer, my history is provocative – in addition I cannot help that I was born to tell stories, and my works include in various forms the whole of my experience – barring that sorry tale which I feel obliged to recount as soon as I can bear to.

To the country that has harboured and never disappointed me I owe heartfelt thanks. Having reached the age at which I must acknowledge the accidents that can befall in the midst of life, I am concerned lest I have not broadcast far and wide my gratitude to Italy, beauteous land, land of beauties, cradle of art and genius, and allevi-ator of the grief with which I have recently been afflicted. – The death of my second child, sweet-est of love children, my darling Allegra, seems to disturb the balance of nature – a father ought not to outlive his daughter – the injustice weighs on me and deepens my inclination to low spirits. And then the death of Shelley reminds my melancholia that no one is immortal. Shelley was more to me than our friendship indicated – he was the lone *colleague* I could abide, for the inky tribe on the whole is savage and fit only to be shunned – and aristocratic writers of merit do not grow on trees, while Philistines do not attract me even if they are wreathed in strawberry leaves. – He will not die, of course, his work will not be subject to mortality – but that his body should ever have been lifeless, his soul departed, his vitality extinguished, and his corpse actually reduced to ashes by a fire which I had personally lit, these are the almost incredible facts now applying to Shelley, who seemed of all people an exception to the rule of human destiny. Italy soothes sore hearts – its sun and oranges are healing – and for its aid to convalescence, in so far as I have convalesced, I must thank again.

Gratitude cannot stop so soon – I have more to thank for – three persons, to be pedantic – my relations with whom are half the last of my stories, the persons are female, and I cannot lump them together since each is like no one else, and, tho' physical love is wrongly said to be a *cliché* and all cats to be grey in the dark, the sensations that each inspired in me were perfectly different. The common denominator of all three was, and remains, matrimony – they were and still are other men's wives. – Adultery suits me – I will not be hypocritical about it – it suits men who do their work at home – it spares us domesticity – and, after all, and I say so to smooth the feathers of respectable womanhood, it leads to our idealisation of a faithful wife and a settled home. Luckily from my point of view, Italians recognise no mundane barrier to romance and passion – they have their religion which affords them the chance to confess their sins and obtain absolution.

To describe two of the three exactly would be indiscreet and a mean recompense for their favours. The first was the prettiest of songbirds where everybody sings, and took me in and nursed me through the illnesses of one sort and another that were my experience of the English Disease, caught from sham puritans and the unfair sex. The second stole me from the first – I was the instigator of the theft – a sight of her on an Italian afternoon moved me to the infidelity of the offer of an assignation – and then we belonged to each other in all but name – temporarily. One restored me to health, which I needed for the second – one sucked the poison from my wounds and restored my faith in the gentleness of some women; – the other was a goddess of the corporeal kind, an Amazon Queen, stronger than the majority of men, configured in such a way as to give and receive the maximum amount of pleasure, and capable of courage and devotion that knew no bounds.

Their husbands I must celebrate in passing, since they *understood* and they forgave the happiness I inadvertently brought into their houses, and, as wit would have it with reference to their modes of earning their livings, they returned my compliments in the generous Italian fashion by *draping* me and providing my daily *bread*.[2]

The second young lady exhausted me. As Marian Jones taught me the ABC of love, so

---

[2]The husband of Marianna Segati was a draper by trade, and the husband of Margarita Cogni, La Fornarina, was a baker.

with M—a I graduated and won my scholarship – we ran through the gamut of passion – and for a change the inevitable end of our carnality was not bitter. Granted, hearts are not always so clever as bodies – she did not like to be told the time had come to terminate our sleepless Venetian siestas and nocturnal gymnastics by the light of the stars – she proved herself capable of jealousy, possessiveness and suicidal inclinations – I had had enough of that sort of thing, and had to appeal to her husband to relieve me of her company. In truth she was the inferior of the great ladies of England by a mile or two, but infinitely superior in her unselfishness and recognition of my essential needs. She cursed me not, she loved me sufficiently to do as I pleased – and I thank her for being an *exception* to all the usual female regulations.

Other matters were on my mind, Greece and its struggle to regain independence, for example – and I fully intended to give love a respite and a rest. But one cannot remember everything. I forgot that a man is never so susceptible as when he drops his guard and thinks he is out of reach of danger. I met a pretty lady, a girl exquisite in every department – a face that could launch two thousand ships, a bosom made to over-excite babies, a waist that a wasp would envy, hips as kissable as lips, white hands with pink fingernails, and feet as tiny as trotters – and she was armed with every weapon against which I have no defence. She was a lady married to a senior gentleman who had other irons in the fire, she was refined, she was as far as it is possible to be from trade, she had literary tastes, *adored* my poetry as is only possible for a female with nothing particular to do, and was not fulfilled to the brim by matrimony. How could I resist her?

The past tense applies to our meeting – to nothing else – and high Italian society does not insist on concealment and whispers as do low English morals. She reciprocated my feelings – or was it vice versa? – and I became her *cavaliere serviente*, a role generally recognised and sanctioned so long as conveniently ambiguous rules are obeyed – in consequence of which, because so many people are now in the know, I can reveal her name, Contessa Teresa Guiccioli. As a result I was almost convinced that the ultimate gift had been bestowed upon me, considering I had attained the ideal which is supposed to be unattainable. She suited me exactly, she was sometimes with her husband and thus enabled me to recoup my forces and to work, she was my Egeria, and with her warm soft limbs around me I belatedly made the acquaintance of happiness.

Alas, fame bears within itself the seed of ingratitude. Not only are writers apt to drink to excess and whore themselves into trouble, they reach up for fame and do down their writing. – What I have done to mine is for others to say, but, certainly, no sooner was I aware of the goodness of the time in question than I began to tire first of the donkey work of dealing with publishers and mechanicals, with correspondence that increased in line with the number of my publications, and secondly of adulation. – Ungratefulness almost prompts me to claim that praise was as unwelcome as blame – I could stomach neither. – Right or wrong, after Teresa and I had settled into our delightful rut, I suspected a falling off in my verses – the stimulus of new love was subsiding, the bright sharp colours became more of a background – and each day, when my hand ached from scrawling irritable letters to Murray and a few dozen refusals of invitations to feasts and *soirées*, I entertained a negative wish that I was obscure and penurious and alone with my Muse in a remote tenement.

A mortifying episode failed to inspire. My love and I were *delicto-ed in flagrante* by the third point in our triangle, the husband, il Conte, who was supposed to be counting his shekels in Ravenna – the services rendered by a *serviente* were not expected to be obviously comprehensive – and I was subjected to a lecture not to my taste and forced to promise to ration my attentions and practise more discretion. – A rift in our lute, that metaphor, would understate the effects of the interruption. – I rankled somewhat, not least because the danger of fatherhood became acute since we had been apprehended in the attitude of procreation – and the lady begged me not to give her a baby which she would not be allowed to mother and bring up. – Teresa was even more apprehensive that a baby sired by her

110

spouse would be suspected of being mine – she was obsessed by precautions and prophylactics – which were not exactly conducive to adulterous joy and satisfaction.

My thoughts therefore strayed from their customary directions – toward acting upon the principles of my poetry and supporting liberty in a different form from the liberties I had been granted by the opposite sex. Greece sought my assistance, which I found hard to refuse – the politics I had espoused from my youth could be pursued in Grecian context – a spark of enthusiasm was rekindled, and a more worthwhile cause could be embraced than the one or the two that were beginning to weigh a trifle heavy.

I hope I have set the scene that exerted influence over my meeting with the lady I shall call by the evocative name of Eve. We met at a populous gathering of lovers of music – music, too – to listen to a tenor gargling the songs of Venice. Teresa was in Ravenna – my lonely eye noted a young woman with unusual looks – dusky complexion, dark frowning eyebrows, aquiline features and fierce expression – and formed the impression that she was original and probably not pleasant. After the music I was *attacked* by a regiment of the opposite sex, and at length succeeded in beating a partial retreat. By accident on my part or by design on hers, Eve and I confronted each other – the symbolic element of the confrontation was that I stood with my back to a wall.

Our strange conversation went thus –

Eve – My name is (she provided her surname).

B. – Madam, you are direct.

Eve – Sir, are not you direct?

B. – Well, madam, I shall give you my name directly.

Eve – I know it, sir. You are the poet. Before we go further, I should tell you I do not like poetry, which falsifies and misleads.

B. – You have strong opinions, madam. I would guess that in poetry and in society you confuse falseness with good manners. Anyway, we are unlikely to go anywhere in the light of your views.

Eve – To be direct is not rude in my book.

B. – Are you a writer, madam? Oh dear, I shall take to my heels without more ado if you are.

Eve – (with grudging smile) I am the wife of a diplomat.

B. – It has not made you diplomatic.

Eve – He is too far distant to rein in my impulses. But I make no apology for being myself.

B. – Where is your husband, madam?

Eve – He has been recalled to London. I am here with colleagues of his, and must now find them. Goodbye, Lord Byron.

Some days later I received an invitation to a supper in the apartment where Eve lived. Curiosity took me there – I was curious to see the man who had dared to marry a girl with so sharp a tongue and with the nerve to provoke a *famous* poet and unwed peer with a reputation for promiscuity. He was not present – Eve was entertaining the Diplomatic Corps on his behalf

112

– by no means an amusing conglomeration of guests – and in consequence of the only thing she said to me, that I was the plum in the pudding of her party, I yielded to the temptation to leave without delay.

That would have been that for me, if fate for once had stayed its hand. Scene Two began out of doors, in a deluge of rain – Venice a mist of wetness – I was returning from an appointment in my gondola, and Eve on a bridge saw and waved to me. – I stopped. She was far from her home, I allowed that I was not shocked by her request for assistance, and took her to my palazzo. She was wet through but denied it, she said she would be glad just to wait till the storm subsided, and I had the fire built up in my salon and gave her some wine to warm her. The time was afternoon, candles were lit, we found ourselves in a situation that put ideas into my head if not obviously into hers, moreover the storm grew wilder and, noticing that she was literally *steaming*, I rang for servants to take her to a room, find her something dry to wear, and bake her clothes in an oven or do whatever should be done to wet clothing. She returned in one of my dressing-gowns, laughing at her train and the sleeves that hid her hands, and her previous direct talk took a more intimate turn.

She was against matrimony as well as poetry. Her husband *I* had better call Timothy, tho', according to his wife, he was honoured more by God, as the name signifies, than by anybody else. Marital relations had been a disappointment to her – how could she have known that she and Timothy were made of such very different flesh and blood? – And she could not altogether renounce her liberal style of life and her idea that women should be allowed certain freedoms. She dreaded motherhood and incarceration in her home until it was too late to express herself.

I had heard it before, it titillated nonetheless – her unbending to confide in me was a compliment, the more affecting for being unexpected. At some stage she was warm enough to roll up her sleeves that were mine, and I saw tantalising brown upper arms, and, when she rearranged herself on my sofa, a naked thigh was momentarily visible. But she appeared not to be trying me deliberately, she frowned more than she flirted, and was rather startled when I rang for servants to escort her to a room where she could change into her own clothes, and again when I summoned a public gondola to carry her home – my private one is recognisable, and for her sake and for my own she should not be seen leaving my premises in it after dark.

None of us know much, if anything – but experience is a sort of knowledge, however youth may deny it – and my experience assured me that Eve would not permit our acquaintanceship to stop at the point already reached – she might have confided in me impersonally, as if thinking aloud and without ulterior motive, but it was now clear to me, clearer than it had been when she ran me to ground *directly*, that, as women will, she had already made up her mind to conquer or be conquered with a minimum of preamble.

A host of reasons reminded me that discretion is the better part of valour. They were, by name, Teresa, my sanctuary, notwithstanding her absence in Ravenna, and foolish Claire Clairmont, who never forgave me for giving in to her and letting her have what she wanted, ultimately the penalty and the reward of sin, my daughter Allegra. – For my poetry, sanity, health, to spare myself embarrassment and the ugly sound of shrill reproaches, to remain without the burden of responsibility for a bastard, and because of my duty to my talent, I should definitely flee to Tom Tiddler's Ground, where I would be untouchable. It was not as if I were concussed by the lady's charm – at first sight she had impressed by her sulkiness, and she was certainly no sweet talker. The trouble was – and is – that bad habits, not broken, get worse – I had become addicted to risk. Eve had displayed attractions that were not on show in society, she was evidently beginning to follow in the footsteps of her most famous forebear and namesake, and I awaited her next move with mingled interest and alarm.

She wrote to me. I had expected a missive – surely she would not venture to beard me in my lair. She was out of sorts, she wrote, she lacked company, and would be at home at nine o' clock on such and such a day. I chose to think there would be other people present, but there were not – I had suspected it – we were alone, for she herself opened the door to me. She led me to her empty drawing-room, where I accused her of kidnapping me with false pretences, to which she answered brusquely that she understood I was an expert at entertaining ladies. No longer a lady in the singular, I corrected her – now only ladies in the plural, I dared not entertain the opposite sex unless it was in a gaggle – therefore I must leave her before regret took precedence and both our reputations were ruined. She would not have it – she flared up and said she could not be bothered with the tinkle of tea-spoons, referring either to social rituals or the preliminaries of amorousness – and she was sick of having to be always on her best behaviour in order to advance her Timothy's career – and I must sit down and stay with her or she would be cross with me.

She was not ordinary, and seemed to deserve my limited co-operation. We talked in a stilted manner for some minutes. As usual I refused to answer her questions about my work – they were too conventional considering she was a confessed loather of literature – and she also issued a refusal to chat with this exchange –

Eve – My interest is biology.

B. – Human biology?

Eve – Mainly entomological.

B. – Beetles excite you?

Eve – Not as you imply.

B. – What position does human biology occupy in your list of interests?

Eve – Change the subject, if you will, my Lord – you tease me.

B. – Well, I am not alone in that.

Eve – Enough, sir!

But she did not mean it – human biology was top of her list – it was soon established. We were ranged at a distance from each other, and she fetched an album of her paintings of butterflies and sat close to me to show me *her* art. I broke the pointless spell of formality by saying that the scent of her distracted me from appreciation of her handiwork. She then begged me not to repulse her loneliness – and her whole personality was translated into a softer appealing libidinous model – in the manner of some women ready for love, as experienced men would agree. The temptation was sudden and strong – I had not thought she possessed an unferocious side – but I stood up and showed her another side of myself, that which women have often called cruel.

No, said I, she was presumptuous, had cornered me without encouragement, had forgotten my age and dignity and her fidelity to her Timothy, whose misplaced trust in his wife was not my fault. – I fairly vented on her my own mixed feelings – I was otherwise engaged, I disclosed – I had a mistress beyond compare to whom I was more faithful than she, Eve, appeared to be – a mistress more desirable than she was, and more agreeable – and I would not play the gigolo to any starved wife in need of a square meal – and she had been misled in thinking I was hers for the asking.

I concluded in the expectation of tears, more pleas, shrieks of anguish, rage in action, and was again surprised. – She was not put off or particularly put out – she continued to gaze at me with that yearning receptive expression transforming her bony features and sallow cheeks into an almost beautiful mask with languorous eyes, rosy cheeks and full lips. – And she spoke to me tenderly, reclining against the cushions on the sofa and saying, *Sir, I have nothing on underneath the rag I wear.*

No, I repeated, shaking my finger or even my fist at her – she was shameless and was not to behave so loosely – at which she began to draw up her skirt. I made to leave her, she followed me laughing. I fear that I joined in, laughing too and licensing her behaviour, and escaped through the front door without physical contact. Before I was in the roadway I heard her cry, *It is not over, Lord Byron* – words with which I could not disagree – words that hung over my head like the Sword of Damocles in the next days.

I could not avoid her. She was included in all the Diplomatic revels. And I did not leave Venice. Thus the plot thickened.

One evening we were seated next to each other at a supper – our host was French, had recently arrived, did not know the niceties of Venetian society, and would have incurred the wrath of Contessa Guiccioli for placing me beside a young unhusbanded Englishwoman with some physical attractions. – We conversed for a change – I pumped her for information about herself, which is usually given with plea-sure – we must have been thought to be getting on well – and in a sense we were. – But she looked at me as women do look at a man with whom they have had any intimate intercourse – with a softening expression and hints of humour and watchfulness, as if poised to take advantage of the slightest sign of weakness or defeatism on his part – and the result was a tension between us, stimulating from one point of view, her point of view, ominous from mine.

She told me she was the daughter of a doctor and a blue-stocking, breeding consistent with her character. Where did she obtain her dusky complexion and the facial cast of an American Indian? She laughed – her teeth were whiter than white because of her dark skin – and said that her father had begun his medical career in India, and that English people out there often acquired a resemblance to the natives. Was it not her mother who had passed on the Asian tint to herself? She scolded me for my slander and cyni-cism, and claimed that her mother had always been beyond reproach. Did she then take after her father? She was amused by my insolence, and the collapse of her stern features had charm. When did bugs enter into her existence? She studied butterflies, not bugs, and both she and her mother loved their colours and pitied the shortness of their lives.

And Timothy, was he another butterfly lover? Not at all, and I was not to poke fun at him. What was he like, tall and handsome, short and hirsute? He was a decent man, not spoilt beyond hope, not rich and arrogant. Was she drawing a comparison between her husband and myself? Not necessarily, unless the cap fitted. She had a sharp tongue, said I, and must mind where it might cut. She answered with a meaningful glance that she could desist from sharpness and be malleable and amenable.

Our flirting was mild – or would have been if it had stopped there – but I had to talk to the neighbour seated on my other side, a gargantuan Marchesa with exclusive interest in fodder – and while I watched the Marchesa munching Eve placed her hand on my thigh under cover of the table cloth – and I could not engage in a wrestling match without providing news that would be soon received and not welcomed in Ravenna. –

I allowed myself to be angered by the girl and as soon as it was possible to leave the table I turned my back on her, but she caught my arm and said *Please let us meet again*, adding that she promised not to frighten me – luckily this in an undertone. – I could not let it pass and hissed at her that tho' I was not a coward I had no desire to pursue our acquaintanceship – then left the house, hoping never having to trespass by a single centimetre into the *Garden of Eden*.

Unfortunately by the witchcraft innate in women Eve had stolen my memory – I had now forgotten that love can be slow poison – and even failed to remember that Adam set a bad example by at last eating the apple. I watched and waited, and even derived amusement from my favourite form of humour, IRONY – for here was I, almost at bay, after being hunted by a nobody ill-bred and possibly with coloured blood in her veins – Byron the great seducer and whorer, the toast of *boudoirs* large or small in a number of countries, brought to a standstill by a chit who undertakes not to frighten him with her propositions – what topsy-turvy world had I strayed into? And what would be said by Lady Caroline Lamb, Lady Byron, my spouse who could not abide me, by my Contessa and sundry other notabilities, if they should ever discover me in such a discreditable position? Where was my precious independence and my pride – that I could not walk away from the city I shared with Eve and have done with the sordid business?

The irony of the reversal of roles reached back to the *baptism* of my manhood. Marian Jones did not find me choosy – Marian captured me without a struggle, despite her age, lack of beauty, immemorable quality and her husband – I was all for Marian, but scrupled to lend myself to Eve, who might be not much but was a lot more than that poor old *schoolmistress* making up for lost time. Ah well, fate was pleased to see me stand on my head – and I was resigned to hanging about until it decided to bring the curtain down on the comedy.

To do otherwise would be difficult from viewpoints already taken into consideration. Teresa would smell a rat if I deserted my Venetian post – Italian girls are born with insight into the minds of men – and not only minds – and the deepest distrust of their sisters and their sex. She knew my history too well – anyway she would be hard to persuade that in her absence nothing whatsoever, nothing of more than passing interest for herself, happened. I would lie low, resist the blandishments of the biologist, risk no fisticuffs with Timothy, and urge my Contessa, my Lady in all but name, to return to Venice not in a hurry – hurry would ring alarms in her pretty ears – just with minimum delay. – For I had lost my taste for battles in bedrooms, and my eagerness to act the pig in the middle – I would not squeeze into the mould of poets, sick with love of everybody and mostly with their precious selves – to continue to be a ladies' man was not the aspiration of the remainder of my days – unwonted wisdom would be the compensation of my older age.

So I argued or hoped – and the plight of Greece claimed more of my attention.

But cursing Eve was by no means the equivalent of committing her to oblivion. While over-rating my power to halt or at least slow down the action of the drama, I under-rated the inventiveness of Cupid and the wicked hilarity of other gods and goddesses. Carnival was approaching, after all – I should have guessed that pomposity was about to be punctured by love and jokes of every description.

An invitation reached me to attend an evening of *tableaux vivants* at the Fenice Theatre. These fashionable performances show gentlemen and ladies apeing the figures in popular paintings – on the stage they appear for several minutes in the apparel of the painted figures – *still lifes*, or as still as society personages can be – applauded by claques of their friends and relations. – The common run of aristocrats are never slow to prove how vulgar they can be, poses are second nature to them, and admiration is their breath of life, whatever its source. Therefore, as on previous occasions, I tore up the card and threw it in the waste-paper basket.

But a day or two later I received a second invitation to the same event, bearing the scribbled message *I challenge you to recognise me.* As a result, wishing the word *challenge* had never been coined, I attended at the Fenice and sat through half a dozen *tableaux*, incapable of hiding my yawns. Then, after a long-drawn-out pause for scenery to be rearranged, the curtain was raised to reveal a verdant scene and a couple underneath an apple tree with a snake curled around its trunk. The man and the woman were as naked as the snake – scarcely a thread of apparel visible – and modesty only preserved by a combination of attitude and shadow – the picture recreated was by one of the Bellinis entitled *The Temptation of Adam*. And Eve was imitated by Eve, disguised by the mask of Columbine – Adam wore Harlequin's cod-piece.

I was inspired to join in the general clapping, which was deserved and surely genuine owing to the beauty of the female physique – in my own case, also, because I was surprised that my Eve – or Timothy's – was perfect in all the relevant particulars. Not merely her proportions must have done justice to the artist's ideal, tho' I was actually ignorant of the picture in question, but her tinted skin from head to toe had a peculiar charm, her body was at once and obviously lithe and sensual, and her pose with the apple in her outstretched hand explained exactly why Adam had taken the unfortunate bite.

My resolutions melted, I took my stand by the Stage Door, and when Eve appeared said that I had recognised her without difficulty, to which she replied suggestively that I had not yet reason to be certain. – At that my excitement subsided, my scruples homed in on me again, and having paid her a compliment or two I bade her good night. – How was she to reach her house, she exclaimed, was I to let her drag her skirts through the gutters, was that how lords behaved to ladies? I offered to transport her in my gondola, irritation with both of us now uppermost – and our voyage not so much through the water as through contentiousness ensued.

She was intent on kissing me or being kissed

– I excused myself before too much damage was done with the lie that my gondolier was the greatest gossip in town and devoted to my Contessa. She fished for compliments – what did I think of various parts of her anatomy – I qualified my praise of her beauty by referring to the luck of Timothy.

Was she better or worse to look upon than Teresa Guiccioli, how did their necks, breasts, hips and the dimensions of their stomachs compare? – I was fool enough to say she was a wanton hussy who would get herself whipped if she was not careful. Would I like that, she inquired, would it excite me, had she excited me in the theatre? – I reminded her that I was at least her senior by a decade and a half and that female flesh was yesterday's news to me. In that case, says she, I must not abandon her in her overwrought state to a sleepless night, I must in charity come into her parlour and talk to her until she was as calm as I seemed to be – well, for ten minutes, I say, regretting my weakness, the more so when she murmured with a giggle *Five would do*.

Her amorousness increased in her front hall – she impatiently offered me more than the apple she had held out to another man – and I cannot pretend I was impervious – the pincer movement of her stern public countenance and the sweet surrender of her features into laughter and license was almost too much for me – besides, the trap was baited by her recent revelations at the Fenice – and old habits die hard – and there is no aphrodisiac so potent as novelty.

125

But I rejected her wooing – kept her at arm's length or nearly – pushed her into a chair for one and told her the cautionary tale of Claire Clairmont, who had as good as raped me – or should I write as bad as raped me? – for the fruits of her womb were sorrow, bitterness and death. She – Eve – was another apprentice to a career of adultery, and should learn a lesson from an old hand instead of making mistakes that were avoidable and often irreparable. I reminded her of a fact of life not commonly known either by virgins or young wives, that behind every drawn blind, bedroom screen, locked door, lurked a baby eager to join in the fun. Yes, yes, I was well aware that there is more than one way to skin a cat; but I also had experience of the difficulty of excluding a baby determined to be made – the passion that is thought to justify adultery is in every sense a slippery slope – and a baby will take advantage and slide into a punitive position *en route* to becoming a millstone. Finally, I hoped to conclude, the danger of conception on the one hand and the absence of Timothy on the other formed an obstacle quite insuperable in reality, if not in her self-indulgent fantasies – I was not in the mood to father another child, and she should be afraid of presenting her spouse with issue that was illegitimate and could be his male heir.

I urged one further point as it were in self-defence. I was not old, except by reference to my short-lived forebears – I felt a thousand years older than she was – my blood was cold in comparison with hers – I had had too much of that of which she had had too little – and what made her think she could count on receiving all that she desired from myself? She was one of many who misunderstood me – I was not a seducer *of* women, I was ever seduced *by* them – and the tense was changing, from I *had been seduced* to I *would no longer be* – she therefore ought to let me depart in peace.

She was sufficiently discouraged by my lecture to raise no physical objections to being left alone, she merely hurled verbal accusations at the back of my head – tease, liar, hypocrite, coward, to all of which, in a just world, I would have had to plead guilty.

Early the next day I fled Venice and sought refuge in Ravenna.

La Contessa welcomed me with surprise and increasingly difficult questions in her lovely eyes. Was I not ill, was I well, why was I not in Venice, what had happened, what was wrong? I essayed to prove by the warmth of my embrace that I was with her because I could not do without her – but she said she could smell another woman on my clothes and even on my skin. Her feminine response to these suspicions was competitive – she demanded love on the instant with unusually savage force, and would not take no for an answer to her request for repetition. Reversion to the topic of events in Venice led to my again being called a liar, and she threw in extra terms of abuse, devil, for example. She was not the woman to fail intuitively to sense that other features interposed themselves in my imagination between her face and mine, and she expressed her degree of dissatisfaction by breaking a few cups and saucers when passion was temporarily spent.

After two or three days and nights she had more or less exorcised the ghost of Eve – her differences charmed me to a nearly exclusive extent. – I was excited by her open expression without the capacity to scowl, by the whiteness of her skin, by her sexuality which was refined and subtle, neither earthy nor brusque, and her naturally pacific temperament. The Count was not in residence at this period – I had the run of his house as well as his wife – and she in her grass widowhood and I beyond the reach of snakes and schemers achieved a kind of contentment. But I was never Darby and she was young and desirous of cooling her blood in the Mediterranean way, she was nothing like Joan. – The twofold consequences were that my *ungrateful* spirit still pined for what was not *hackneyed*, even as my body contradicted the idea that I had the energy to engage in sexual antics with anyone else.

I put forward to my dearest one the plea of work waiting to be done. It was true – I had deadlines to meet, correspondence to attend to, Greece to liberate, not to mention a matter that women will not regard as vital, making money to pay for the staff of life. She did not believe me but knew better than to try to stop me – instead of locking me in and keeping the key, she chose to exert control over my activities in Venice by saying she would join me there as soon as possible – any day – perhaps tomorrow. Inevitably, to prove her love, she wept over our parting, said I was breaking her heart, and forced me to promise her a farewell scene in her orangery before I set out.

It occurred in the morning amidst orange trees and the heady scent of orange blossom. Teresa greeted me bravely and prolonged our embraces – I demurred, but allowed her to lead me towards a long chair on the principle of least said soonest mended – she was determined to *milk* our goodbyes of every emotion – and I have to confess, whether or not it is gentlemanly to do so, that in possibly the most enviable of all positions in the whole of Italy I performed without enthusiasm, mechanically, and ardent only in the hope of getting it over. What stirred the pot, what stimulated, was the intrusion of il Conte into the proceedings.

He had the good manners to turn his back on us and walk away – he belonged to the older school of the etiquette of realism – and he might have been growing accustomed to it, since it had happened once before. I told Teresa that I would deal with him, but she pretended to be fearful that he would *deal with me* and was determined to protect me like some heroic Roman matron. We adjusted our clothing and entered the salon, where the Count awaited us. As I recall our triangular conversation went thus –

Count G. (in English more broken than spoken) Good morning, Lord Byron.

Lord B. – Good day, sir. I suppose I owe you an apology.

Countess G. – Lord Byron has nothing to apologise for – only I am to blame.

Count G. – (in Italian, which I shall translate, to his wife) My dear, hold your tongue. (To me) I would prefer not to quarrel with you, Lord Byron.

Lord B. – My sentiments exactly, sir – far from quarrelling, I would like to thank you for your hospitality in a general sense.

Countess G. – (Betraying her disappointment that we were not fighting over her honour) Thank God no blood is to be spilt!

Count G. – (To his wife) I do not spill my blood for unworthy causes. Please leave the room, so that I can reach an understanding with your *cavaliere*.

Countess G. – (To her husband) But he will leave without my seeing him again or saying goodbye.

Count G. – (To his wife) You have already bidden our gentleman guest goodbye with unconventional warmth.

Countess G. – (To her husband) You are cruel! (To me) Until I reach Venice, beloved!

Lord B. – (To Countess G) Do as the Count tells you. Au revoir!

Count G. – (When we are alone) May I offer you refreshment, milord?

Lord B. – A glass of brandy, if you please, sir.

Count G. – Brandy is often necessary after exercise so early in the day.

Lord B. – Very true, sir – at other hours, too.

Count G. – Indeed! Lord Byron, my wife is stronger than I thought she would be when I married her, and she is less occupied than I am. Your friendship with her and ability to entertain her does not go unappreciated. My family is honoured by the interest of such a famous man.

Lord B. – You are generous, sir. And I wish English husbands had half your common sense and your tolerance.

Count G. – Thank you for your compliment. May I ask how you think we are to live without embarrassment?

Lord B. – You have nothing much to fear from me, sir. I shall do my utmost to prevent accidents happening again. And I can assure you that fidelity is not my strongest suit. Anyway, passion is a shooting star. (This had to be explained pedantically to the Count.) As you may have heard, sir, I sympathise with the Greek people who are trying to be rid of the Turkish yoke. Correspondence is an unwieldy instrument with which to wage a war – I foresee a removal of myself to Greece before too long.

Count G. – You are gallant in all respects, Lord Byron. But my wife and I will miss you, naturally.

Lord B. – I could echo that statement if you were to cut it in half.

Count Guiccioli asked me to elucidate the latter sentence, but I hummed and hawed, not liking to rub it in that his wife would probably do most of the missing, and at length I was able to climb into my conveyance with a sigh of unqualified relief.

Love was the last thing on my list of Venetian priorities. I dealt with issues that could not be postponed, and feared the warning signal of another attack of melancholia. My private life disagreed with me, I looked back at a trail of witless damage and resolved to mend my ways or cut my throat. Reunion with Teresa was not anticipated with pleasure – she had as it were chained me to her skirt by threatening to return and spy on me without warning – and I loved the dove in her, not the despot. As for Eve, I wanted none of her mixture as before.

My hypocrisy was unconscious, tho' now I see and own up to it. How could I have convinced myself that Eve had ceased to exist for me when I avoided the streets by day and used only commercial gondolas? Secretly, in my deeper depths, I was playing for time and for Timothy – she would not nag me into her bed if her husband was already there.

Yet by deliberately lengthening my hours of attendance on poetry and papers I sharpened my appetite for recreation, and Carnival was in the offing. Hobhouse and friends of his were expected in Venice, and I issued an invitation to the whole crew to dine *chez* Byron. They duly arrived, masked as appropriate and having struggled through the crowd without mishap, and we caroused together as men only can when women are not tugging at their sleeves. – It was like old days at Newstead, when we were free of care – except that we consumed more alcohol and were no longer of an age to withstand its worst effects. By midnight my guests wished for nothing but to stop the world spinning by getting to bed. But brandy and I were used to each other – I was not so intoxicated as not to know I was restless and far from sleep – restless and lonely. – I caught a glimpse of myself not as the King of Hearts, rather that *cliché* on legs, a middle-aged bachelor without attachments – and to escape the depressing vision I opened my front door in hopes of escape into anonymity, of losing myself in the multitude, amidst the music, laughter and love that was not my business.

Strangers barged me, Harlequins and Columbines buffeted, noise deafened, the kissing saddened, and I turned for home in order to seek further comfort in the *spiritual* arms of Bacchus – and Eve stood before me.

It was like an apparition – I somehow knew in a flash that I had summoned her – that I had ached and was aching for her – and my heart rose into my throat and tears started from my eyes. She wore Columbine's dress with the tight-waisted coatee and full skirt, and no doubt the triangular 'modesty' in the colours of Harlequin-ade in place, where it had been during the *tableau vivant* – and she was smiling up at me, while tears of sympathy, matching mine, rolled down her cheeks from under her mask. We clasped each other, we collapsed upon each other – I could not speak – I had nothing that needed saying – and she was mumbling that she had been certain I had not deserted her and that we were bound to meet again. – And she held my hand and repeated those words which can be sweeter than any, *Come with me.*

She was leading me towards her house, and I retained enough presence of mind to ask *Where is Timothy?* Still abroad, she replied over her shoulder, home tomorrow, she added meaningfully – *home tomorrow, did you hear?* I heard and understood – we entered her house – she removed her mask and showed me her hard-boned features with their soft-hearted expression, her infinitely black eyes and her lips pink against the darker skin. We mounted her stairs, she with some difficulty owing to the size of her skirt, and at the top, in her moonlit drawing-room, when we embraced, she again complained of the inconvenience of her skirt and in a minute had stepped out of it. From there to nothing was but a short distance – her jacket finished on the floor, a nether garment was discarded, by the time we reached her bedroom she was in the altogether – and she was kissing me and tugging at my buttons.

Oh, I admired her, even objectively – I had admired them all – desire lends enchantment without fail – but my feelings for Eve were

heightened by my abstinence and by the dissat-
isfactions of Ravenna – moreover I was well
versed in the lesson gentlemen have to learn, to
wit, that pleasure is extractable from giving in to
the ladies and pain is apt to be suffered for
refusing to do so. – I turned her this way and
that, as if she had been a statue, and handled
her with care – I revelled in postponement while
she undressed me with equal sensuality. But at
last the lump in my throat dissolved, and sense
did its best to enter into our frolic.

I asked rhetorically if she knew, we knew,
what we were doing.

B. – I must love you too much to harm you.

Eve – Love is not harmful.

B. – You are optimistic. Do you forget conse-
quentiality?

Eve – A long word, a writer's word, not used by
lovers.

B. – Be serious for a second. Do you want a
child?

Eve – Yours, yes, if destiny decrees it.

B. – Timothy might not take it lying down, as
they say.

Eve – He can take it in no other way – I have
to do all the work when we lie together.

B. – Concentrate, my dear – a baby is no joke.

Eve – Timothy returns tomorrow – I can be sure
that paternity of my child, should I have one,
will never be established beyond the shadow of
doubt.

B. – The wiles of women would not spare you
his doubtfulness.

Eve – You forget, sir – I may abandon Timothy or murder him, and land on your doorstep.

B. – No, no – you must not run away with the idea that I would open my door to you – poets do not marry if they are clever or if they have once made the mistake of marrying – that is law for me.

Eve – You love me little, I think.

B. – Not in the matrimonial manner – you will end on the streets if you divorce Timothy or he divorces you – I warn you lovingly.

Eve – We were better before we began to misuse our tongues.

B. – I hope you are not more saucy than understanding.

Eve – To bed, sir – look at me now, in this attitude, or do you prefer that, or another? Forget your words, my love, we will communicate clearly without them.

I followed instructions, or tried to. The combination of Ravenna, exhaustion of mind and body, brandy, and our talk which included torturous implications for me and probably for both of us, robbed me of vigour. She was patient, she blamed herself, she said she had heard that it was a quite common experience for men. – But my pride was wounded – I shrank the more for having given cause to be considered common – humiliation was the opposite of arousing – I apologised for disappointing her and bowed myself out of her house as quickly as I could.

Explanation would have sounded like excuses, and compounded impotence with pathos. I could not lower myself so far as to beg for her indulgence – she had been the beggar, I would not borrow her begging bowl. Our association was different from all others – she was at once too far from me in age, intellect, social standing and practical knowledge, and too near and neighbourly – and I had small trust that she would not turn nasty. Her consolation was acid on my soul, and her serpentine attempts to kiss me better merely reminded me that I had landed myself in a snake pit. Stay with me, she had cried – all would be well, she assured short-sightedly. She saw not much and foresaw less, for instances, negatively, that failure is infectious, that one failure is likely to lead to another, that I would never again expose myself to mortification in her wide open arms, that I could not rely on her discretion, and that cohabitation with her and her husband in the same city would not be possible in future.

A dark day succeeded my blunder in the dark. I was not dead, yet my life seemed to pass in review before my eyes, while I ground my teeth to realise that a nobody of uncertain parentage had been chosen to bring about my downfall – and more to the point, deflect me from my aims and purposes. Was I now to join the self-pitying poets? Was I to be the cause of Teresa's blushes, reproaches, uncertainty, caution? Should I become a monk? Where was I to go?

God had compensated for my crippled foot,

ladies had benefited and in return had given me leave to inflame and provoke them. My talents in two directions had convinced me that I was not only the sixth Baron Byron but a Lord of Creation. Now the tables were turned – my reflection in the mirror might have been a picture entitled The Revenge of Womanhood – I felt as if I had shrivelled from top to toe – and I sank down to dreading a visitation from yet one more injured husband – who really did have nowt to grumble at.

In so far as I could raise my eyes above the unlovely prospect of Timothy, I could acknowledge that Eve was more a symptom than a cause – I would not have given her a second glance if I had not been in a low state, at once sick of fame and fearful it was slipping through my fingers, not sufficiently appreciative of my beautiful mistress, fed up with love as men generally make it, yearning for greener pastures and for fields of battle not merely with publishers, and writhing in the icy grip of melancholy. Eve was a phase of my affliction, maybe – she was the vice that balanced Teresa's virtue – or perhaps I myself chose her to bring my festering soreness to a head.

Timothy arrived in due course. I would not avoid his company, tho' he never would have been a companion of mine. He was a plump pink-faced abbreviation of a man, forcing his voice into the bass register to frighten me and acting the part of dignity affronted. What could I do for him, I inquired.

T. – Listen to me, sir! (He began.) You have alienated the affections of my wife.

B. – The wound, if any, is not deep, sir.

T. – You have taken advantage of my wife in my absence on the order of my superiors, and I have come to call you a blackguard.

B. – Are you desirous of a duel, sir? Well, I am a poet, I do not thirst for blood, and will not fight you. If your object is to kill me, please do so without more erroneous talk. I see you have no sword – there are pistols over on that table, which you are welcome to use.

T. – You mock me, sir. But you are in the wrong, for my wife tells me she loves you now and no one else.

B. – I have not taken serious advantage of your wife – she will not bear my child – there, I have done you the favour of telling you the truth – and will go even further and swear that my truth is true. You and your wife will be bothered by me no more. She is charming in her way, and affectionate, and I advise you not to put your work before your marriage, if you wish to retain her services.

T. – She is changed beyond recognition, my Lord – and I fear I cannot compete with you.

B. – Make her believe that I have left her – and when she has cried her eyes out, get her with child and wait for her to love you a quarter as much as she loves your progeny.

T. – Did you love her, sir?

B. – She acted Eve in the *tableau vivant*, did she inform you? – and she cast me as her Adam. The writer of the Bible understood men, who will always blame the opposite sex for their fall from grace. But I used to have a weakness for women, and cannot be bothered to claim for the umpteenth time that I am the one who has been taken advantage of. Bid your wife adieu from me.

T. – Sir, you forget, my tour of duty in Venice is not at an end – we are bound to meet one another constantly.

B. – Not if I were elsewhere.

T. – Do you plan to return to London? My next posting will be London, Lord Byron.

B. – My destination will be to the east, I imagine.

T. – When do you leave?

B. – Sir, I am impulsive – my present impulse is to be gone without delay – despite many decisions to be taken and arrangements made. I will submit one more thought for your consideration, that the ladies are always ready for a holiday.

T. – You have spoken better than I expected, Lord Byron. Yet I cannot say I am greatly cheered.

B. – Sir, cheerfulness is a rare accomplishment. Happiness in short bursts is achievable, but cheerfulness in the long run is not often sanctioned by the gods. I will stop preaching at this point.

T. – Goodbye, Lord Byron.

B. – Farewell!

I was sorry for Timothy, tho' could not bring myself to say so – he was unfit to be Eve's

140

husband, and his second mistake after marrying her was to leave her alone for weeks in Venice. I did not apologise but should have thanked him, for, insignificant and helpless as he was, he had nonetheless inadvertently suggested a way out of the imprisonment of my difficulties.

I consorted with no one except melancholia – a pretty name for a girl, if the meaning were different – and when the mood had ceased to torment me I returned to my desk and wrote these two additional chapters of autobiography, my introduction to the pleasures of the flesh in my schooldays and the circumstances of my renunciation of the same when I was prematurely past my prime. The writing was fast and furious, and is nearly done – whether or not I ever have the pages copied by a more legible hand remains to be seen – they could not be printed for years to come undoubtedly, and I expect them always to shock the puritans.

I have no more time to waste on my fascinating self or on literary matters, but need to tie up a few loose ends.

The spur to my dashing off revelations not entirely to my credit was the contrast between then and now – the similarities and dissimilarities of a beginning and an end seemed to be worthy of note. Unexpectedly, my guide through these pages has been Jones, my schoolmaster, who would die to know that he and I had something besides his wife in common if he were not already dead. – For he had been in one boat that was sinking, partly thanks to my climbing into it, and I am or could be in another boat of the same build – but the role that fate chose for Jones I cannot suffer, my pride will not let me show how *wrecked* I have been. Poor Jones, never poor Byron! I may spare sympathy for my fellows whose sorrows I was responsible for, because I now know why they cried; – on the stage of the world I will do no more than to chart my voyage on these scraps of paper.

Thank the *bon Dieu* that my melancholy interims are creative. – Yes, I have written more and better when I am down than when I am up – the absence of excitement is an aid to concentration, and red herrings are not spotted in those murky waters. But I shall break my mirror now for good or ill – stop regarding my reflection – and leave it to others, and other generations, to analyse my writing and dissect my soul.

I am soon to go to Greece to serve the cause which has been my Holy Grail ever since I was the oppressed captive of my harsh and stupid mother. Liberty to love and to cease to love has been the object of my manhood to date – for which I have been misunderstood by the female sex and have earned a reputation for wickedness – but that is beside the point – my future services will be rendered to Liberty in the abstract and impersonal. – My contribution to the fight for the freedom of the land that nurtured the greatness of art will not be for my own death or glory – or glory and death, in that order – tho'

I can think of many who will accuse me of base motives – in my heart it is to pay the price of my good and bad luck. I use the word *pay* advisedly – sums of money that agitate my banker have already been handed over to my Greek friends and allies – and, to come down to earth, where I am at home, it has not escaped my thrifty Scotch notice that my *scandalous* scribblings might be sold to defray expenses, if the buyer were rich and powerful enough to put the MS aside for private perusal and a rainy day.

My plans and my mistress, how did they and did they not coalesce? How did the latter respond to the former? Teresa was stricken, she would perish without me, she had had inklings of my intentions, she admired my heroism, she loved me the more for it, she would count the days until she was again in my arms, and she would be utterly faithful to me, save in the matrimonial dimension – ah, how delicious the ambiguity of women, Italian women in particular! Teresa retains her perfection in my eyes, for I know she is partly truthful, and that another part of her realises a break would not be bad for any corner of the eternal triangle – absence might make me fonder, relieve her husband, and reinforce the peaceful element in which she prospers and I have prospered too. I would write to her, yes – and yes, she could have legal power to deal with my business affairs in the meanwhile – and yes again I promised that my pre-occupations were exclusively military – result, she was almost mollified. Here, where she will read it, I will also give my word that she has been the joy of however many years we have been together, that she has made me happier than any other woman, and I live in hopes – deferred, of course – of breathing my last in her embrace.

The tender parts resistant to mollification have been, in the first instance, my poetry – how was I going to write exquisite verses amidst the horror and din of war? I try to convince her that my career in that line is drawing or has drawn to a close, and other interests take precedence. One day she may grasp the fact that as a rule, a rule I did not break, poetry is the province of youth and love in its intensest forms both soulful and physical – she may not choose to see such facts as slighting to herself. – I do believe that I was born to be one of the poets and my verses will live after me – at the same time I recognise that there can easily be too much of a good thing, and that no lover is so fickle as a lover of the literature in vogue. Anyway, I cannot help but feel that my switch from the pen to the sword is suited to my circumstances, all things considered.

The second instance refers to love in action. For the outlay of a single sovereign and the co-operation of an angel of the night, I have proved that the fiasco in the *Garden of Eden* was nothing to do with a permanent disability. But I was and still am unprepared to test myself in the company of a lady in society, where secrets are currency for conversational exchange. Having two reputations to protect, poetical and amorous, I am loath to disappoint Teresa in particular, and leave her a defaced picture of her ever obliging *cavaliere* – and sooner or later to be placed in the pillory and jeered at by my amiable and compassionate fellow human beings. One female in the know, Eve, is more than enough, and she and her Timothy at least have reason not to disclose that she was party to my failure.

The clock ticks on, and I would close these two essays and the decade and a half of my younger life with words of praise and gratitude. – I refer to the female approximations to an ideal, and the fair inspirations of my fame and fortune. You delighted me, you maddened me, you were my everything and my nothing, indispensable and extraneous, heart-breakingly beautiful at one moment and ugly as sin the next, my destiny and my disaster simultaneously. You worshipped me and consigned me to burn in hell, you amused me and bored me to distraction with your unpunctuality and your tears, you never denied yet bullied and blackmailed me if you could, you were my partners, accomplices, colleagues, supports, hindrances, obstacles, enemies. You have talked to me for all these years of love, and I have learned to speak your language – it has been lovers' lane for ever. But whether or not I can share that emotion, understand it, describe it in scientific detail, weigh it, assay it, is a question hard to answer. Lust is not a puzzle, competition is no problem, satisfaction is clear to animals, which are incorrigible dynasts, contentment is universally recognised – where does that leave love? I apologise for my provocative nature, but must confess that I think I have loved my dogs more than my women.